AUTHOR	CLASS
HILTON, J. B.	FICTION RESERVE E
TITLE Mr Fred	No
	18305700

Mr Fred

The setting of this short, powerful mystery is Edwardian Derbyshire. The story is told by Kathy in her old age, but the events she describes took place when she was still a child at school, living in abysmal poverty but cunning, sensitive and beset by pre-adolescent fears, some imaginary, some all too real.

Kathy secretly encounters the mysterious Mr Fred who is being hidden on her father's farm. But why? Who is Mr Fred? What is the truth behind the scandalous rumours about him? Surely it cannot possibly be true that this kindly man is a pervert and a murderer? And why does her dull-witted brother finally murder him? If he did . . .

Kathy—who adores Mr Fred—more than once outwits the formidable Inspector Brunt, who has appeared in three of John Buxton Hilton's previous Derbyshire novels. She is a married woman, prospering in the 1920s—and Brunt has already died of old age—before she finally penetrates to the shock of the truth.

This novel, with its haunting evocation of time and place and its keen analysis of emotions, both infantile and adult, will appeal to many who do not usually reckon to care for suspense novels.

JOHN BUXTON HILTON

Mr Fred

COLLINS, 8 GRAFTON STREET, LONDON WI

William Collins Sons & Co. Ltd
London · Glasgow · Sydney · Auckland
Toronto · Johannesburg

First published 1983
© John Buxton Hilton 1983

British Library Cataloguing in Publication Data

Hilton, John Buxton
Mr Fred. —(Crime Club).
I. Title
823'.914[F]   PR6058.I58

ISBN 0 00 231490 8

Photoset in Compugraphic Baskerville
Made and printed in Great Britain by
William Collins Sons & Co. Ltd., Glasgow

PART ONE

CHAPTER 1

There was something spiteful about the stories that my sister Lilian used to tell us at bedtime. This was largely for my benefit, since she was supposed to keep us in order and I was born to be a scapegoat. When other means failed, she had to rely on avenging skeletons and nameless things that she conjured up through the panels of locked cupboards. I suppose she was hardly to be blamed. When Lilian was sixteen, I was twelve, Emily was eight and Caroline was six. We were a poor family. Lilian's responsibility for us younger ones was heavy. She pinched our bottoms, tweaked our ears and sometimes made a final appeal to our father's belt. Or she called on punishing spirits to come out of the shadows.

Emily and Caroline would believe anything. They never seemed to learn from experience. When our parents came upstairs for the night, my mother always stood for a second and listened at our door. She trod gently, but it was always the same floorboard that creaked, and Lilian would time a terrible moment in the night's tale to coincide with the shifting ray of candlelight under our door, the fanwork of shadows across our ceiling. The little ones thought it was a kind of magic. And even my flesh sometimes crept, grown-up as I was—I do believe that before the First War we were more grown-up at twelve than children are nowadays. Lilian seemed to know in advance when an old can was going to be blown about the yard—always at the right moment to do duty as a rattling chain. And if there was an owl in the spinney, there would be one in her story.

It may seem strange that Mr Fred should have come into my mind that night. It was a long time since we had last set eyes on him. So why should I be thinking of Mr Fred as I lay listening to Lilian, trying to anticipate the muffled footfall on the stair that would be her cue for a scary twist in the tale? She always told her stories in a hoarse whisper; even Lilian was forbidden to talk in bed. But she could have you believing that a whisper was a shout.

I cannot remember what that night's story was about, but I know that there was a horse in it. And I know that I had heard horses' hooves down at the village end of the farm—quite unaccustomed, at that time of night—and my thoughts were straining in different directions. I was waiting for Lilian to bring a horseman, headless no doubt, into her story; and I was struggling to know what was actually happening.

For there had been other things: more clatter than usual downstairs from our parents. One of the boys had called from their bedroom, something I could not catch; and my father had shouted back, gruff and final. When my father called for quiet, even the shadows went deeper.

'There was no horse there, but you could hear one, pounding and panting. And you were rooted to the spot. You couldn't move. It was going to charge right over you. You were going to pass right through it, ice-cold. You couldn't move a limb.'

'You'd be dead,' Caroline said glibly. She'd heard the word often enough, but it had no meaning for her. And I wanted them to stop talking so that I could hear what was going on outside. There was more than one flesh-and-blood horseman coming up along the wall of the Four Acre. I could not remember when we had ever had a visitor at this time of night.

'What was that?'

Lilian shot upright in bed. I thought it was another of her tricks; then I knew that she too was frightened. Caroline pulled the bedclothes up over her head and Emily, who has been something of a coward all her life, started to cry.

'Be quiet! I want to listen!'

Lilian had abandoned her story. She and I knew that there were two riders and that they were coming to our house. Anyone climbing that hill could not be heading anywhere else. The horses pulled up and I heard one of them snort as someone leaned down to undo the gate-fastening. The men were carrying lanterns and the light played in at the edges of our window. Hooves squelched through the mud and litter of the yard.

'Go and look, Kathy.'

That was just like Lilian. If my mother or father had snatched open our door and I was caught standing at the window or keyhole, my punishment would serve as an example. And Lilian would be pretending to be asleep.

But my common sense never was a match for my curiosity. I had pulled plenty of chestnuts out of the fire in my time, including some for Lilian, and been whipped for my pains. But I swung my feet out on to the freezing oilcloth, went to the window, edged aside the curtain. And there were two men in the yard. The night was dark and the play of their lanterns was tantalizing. The light rested for seconds on what they were looking at, but would not stay still for me to see things properly. I caught sight of one of the men, but only for an instant: he had the sort of face that belonged in one of Lilian's stories. He was not very tall and his lamp cast shadows upwards over his features, exaggerating every wart and pimple.

They swung their lanterns so as to take in the farmyard a sector at a time: the dunghill, the well, the kennel. Brindle was raging, and they gave her a wide berth: she would have had pieces out of their legs. The taller man stepped aside to look into the cart shed and try the latch of the shippon. The other came straight up to the kitchen door and hammered, not once, not three times, but continuously. The timbers shook in their frame.

'Open up, Farmer Hollinshead. You have company. Two sets of company, if I am not mistaken.'

A new patch of light picked out a straw-littered triangle of cobbles sloping down to a drainage grid. My parents' bedroom window opened. It was my mother who leaned out, and she was angry.

'Who are you? Stop all that noise. There are eight children asleep in the house—*were* asleep.'

'Police Inspector Brunt and Sergeant Bacon. We have a justice's warrant to search house and grounds.'

'At this time of night?'

'I would prefer to do it without damage. I would be within my rights to break this door down. But we don't want anything like that, do we?'

A familiar streak of light slanted under our badly-fitting door. I tiptoed to stoop to the keyhole. It was a wonder I did not suffer permanent cold in one eye, from the amount of reporting that I did from that vantage point.

My mother had come out on to the landing carrying a candle. We naturally thought of her as quite old, but she was then some years short of forty, tall, stern and prim, but with very clear skin and long black hair loosened about her shoulders. She stood for a moment at the top of the stairs, then I heard her say something to herself in a whisper.

'Oh no! Not asleep!'

She went downstairs and seemed to be having difficulty with the bolts and chain. There was whispering below, then someone came upstairs in stockinged feet. But there was not enough light for me to see more than a shadow pass—a shadow that went into my parents' room.

I heard the last bolt drawn. The door opened and Inspector Brunt came into the house. He did not stop to argue with my mother or to look around downstairs, but came straight up to the landing in his heavy boots, went arrow-straight towards my parents' door and pushed it open. I caught sight of my father, still in bed, his face buried in the pillow.

'Come along, Mr Hollinshead. I need you with me when I search the sheds.'

Then the Inspector wheeled round, and before I knew it, he had snatched open our door. I fell forward over his boots.

'What's this, then? Up late to see the show, are we?'

'Kathy—get back into bed at once!'

That was my mother's voice. If anyone was going to disturb her children, she meant to be on hand. There was a leather strap hanging in the scullery, on which my father sharpened his razor, and I expected it to be put to its secondary use next morning. But somehow that went forgotten.

Inspector Brunt was not put off by having my mother on his heels. He came past me and pulled the sheet from Lilian's face. She gave a little yelp of outrage. Emily was snivelling, Caroline trembling. Then he left us and went into the boys' room. I heard my father clomp out on to the landing. It was a long time later that I realized that he ought not to have been clomping. He never went upstairs in his boots. He invariably left them downstairs.

For a long time we heard the policemen stamping about the house, and from time to time my father's voice was raised. Then they trooped outside and rattled and banged in the outhouses. I did not dare go to the window again. We lay paralysed, trying to make sense of the noises: the stable, the dairy, the granary. And my father turned his anger against Brindle, who would not stop barking.

Then they all came in again and there was a long palaver in the kitchen. My father's voice was now so loud that I could hear every word. He was going to ride into town the next morning and complain to the Superintendent. But even as a child, I knew that when morning came he would do no such thing. He was a strange man, my father. He would let fly at things while his furies were on him, but his words were fiercer than his actions.

At last the intruders rode away. My mother came up with her candle and looked into our room. But we were pretending—even to each other—that we were asleep.

How long it took my sisters to doze off, I don't know. I lay awake long enough to hear someone come out of my parents' door. Whoever it was moved very quietly across the landing and down the stairs. My hearing was exceptionally sharp through long practice at prying into things that should not have concerned me. I heard the groan of a stair, the brush of a sleeve against the banister.

I knew who it was. There is nothing that calls back the past so vividly as an old and familiar smell. I knew then what had turned by thoughts to Mr Fred tonight. I am over eighty now, but that aroma would still take me back. When Inspector Brunt tore the door open in front of my face, I caught the tang of a brand of pipe tobacco that I shall recognize to my dying day.

Inspector Brunt, of course, thought it was my father's.

CHAPTER 2

It was years before I understood what had happened. My mother and father had played a simple trick, and it had worked, even against the formidable Inspector Brunt. When the door opened on a man in a grey nightshirt, burying his face in my father's pillow, it was not my father that I saw. My father, in his boots, was hiding among the coats and dresses behind the curtain in the corner. He waited long enough for Inspector Brunt to think he had thrown on his clothes, then he clomped down the stairs. Inspector Brunt did not think of visiting the bedroom a second time. It did not occur to him that Mr Fred might be in my parents' bed. But that was where Mr Fred remained until the Inspector and his henchman had ridden off into the night.

So who was Mr Fred?

It might be as well to say something first about who we were ourselves. As well as us four girls, there were four boys. William was seventeen, and had long ago left school. He was working with my father about the farm—or, let us be honest, he was keeping as great a distance between himself and our father as he could contrive. Stanley, at ten, was in the same class at school as myself. Walter, who was four, had not started school yet, but had already moved into the bed with the bigger boys. Thomas, one and a half, was still sleeping in the cot at the foot of my parents' bed.

The children of a large family lead an existence quite apart from the life that their parents know about: a complex of privacies. I do not mean that we were deceitful—except over a few trivialities. But we had our own world. We had our quarrels; we were always bargaining, making and breaking alliances. We had our secret games and our foolish imaginings. The face that we showed to strangers was uniquely ours. And in no way did the spirit of the Hollinsheads assert itself more memorably than on our morning walk to school.

The morning after Mr Fred's visit, we were late setting off. Our parents had overslept and everything was ten minutes behind—ten minutes that wrought havoc with us all. We stood round the table at our plates of bread and lard: there were not enough chairs for all of us, but it was not only poverty that ordained that we should stand to our meals. It was considered a proper discipline. William had graduated to a chair when he started work, Lilian when she became a pupil-teacher.

By a quarter past eight we were strung out in the open air, my mother having inspected fingernails, buttons and bootlaces as we left the house. We filed beside the wall of the cowshed, keeping our feet to the few inches of coarse grass that skirted the drystone wall as far as the gate. You could be caned at school for dirty boots, and we Hollinsheads considered it an unfair disadvantage to have to start off through twenty yards of cattle-stompings. Then we followed the wall of the Four Acre — downtrodden grass, rather than a marked path. And so over the brow and down the Dumble, a shallow and arid dip in the hillside, hardly worth the title of valley or clough. When I remember those scarred masses of lichened outcrop limestone, I still think of artists' pictures of the prehistoric world. There was so much surface rock, so little depth of soil, that in most of our fields it was only sheep who could fend for themselves. Here and there a twisted tree leaned away from the prevailing wind in a gesture of defiance.

By the time we were half way down the Dumble, we were strung out over a fair stretch of country. Stanley was for ever ranging up the flanks of the cleft in quest of insects. Emily and I were dawdling gossipers. Caroline chose this of all mornings to look for cowslips.

'Cowslips!'

Lilian was contemptuous. Six months earlier, Caroline had been praised for taking in a hot, wilting handful that Miss Hargreaves, the infant teacher, had put on the windowsill in one of her precious jamjars. Caroline still had no proper sense of seasons.

'Cowslips in October! Do come on!'

Lilian had more to lose by being late than any of us: Mr Webster did not make allowances, even for pupil-teachers, and Lilian cherished her angelic reputation. She still does.

Once we reached the Waterlow Road we had to stick together, in case we ran into the Wardles or the Ollerenshaws. Three years ago, William's long reach and rocky knuckles had protected us; now we were not ashamed to rely on Lilian's link with authority. Mornings were the most dangerous. The perils of intertribal warfare were always less on our homeward trek. In the afternoon children had their homes to go to. They were looking outwards from the prisonhouse. Unless something had happened during the day that demanded instant revenge, there was seldom a fight that drew blood on the way home.

We were late and of course none of us had a watch, so we could not know how late. We could see the Wardles, stubbing their toes in the stony dust a hundred yards ahead of us, which gave us hope that we still might dead-heat with Mr Webster's whistle. But Caroline was dragging. Lilian gave her two sharp raps across the calves, whereupon she stood stubbornly still and howled. Emily and I took her between us and got her along with the soles of her feet sometimes missing the ground altogether.

We were in time—only just. When we drew in sight of the school, Lilian strode ahead of us. She would not be seen walking with us through the yardgate. She no longer had to wait with us out in the playground in all weathers, but went straight through the porch to receive her orders of the day from Mr Webster.

The day that followed was a terrible one. I could normally hold my own in Mr Webster's classroom. I was never openly rebellious, though this was out of prudence rather than of character. I could average six or seven out of ten when we worked through the yellow, dog-eared arithmetic cards. Today the figures kept slipping away from me, and I made wild guesses rather than drag my pen round the wearisome long multiplications. I was privately astonished at how naughty I was being that day. After the broken night, I was too tired even to try to keep out of trouble.

Half way through the morning, Inspector Brunt came in; came into the big schoolroom, stood talking to Mr Webster, looking round the faces of the class—with an occasional glance sideways at Lilian, who was taking a reading lesson in the gallery. And I do not think that it was my imagination: his eye rested on me several times. Last night I had only seen his face distorted by the shadows from his lantern. Broad daylight did not improve his looks. He had warts and wens and carbuncles and I had heard people say that he used his ugliness to help him in his work. People would tell him what he wanted to know, rather than stay close to those eyes and jowls longer than they need.

I could not hear what was being said, but I could see that Mr Webster's eyes were also wandering from one young Hollinshead face to another. I looked round at Lilian, though I had to slew round in my seat to do so. Her back was towards the rest of us, and up in the gallery she was suffering. There were big lads in her class who were adept at backchat without moving their lips for Mr Webster to see. I did not know whether she was even aware that Inspector Brunt had come in. But I thought she knew, and that she was frozen with fear at the thought of showing him anything but a square-cut view of her shoulders and the back of her head.

I saw Mr Webster shake his head, politely, reluctantly—but firmly. Was he refusing to allow Inspector Brunt to talk to us? Displeasure did not help his looks, either. His eyes fell on me again.

'Katherine Hollinshead—get on with your work!'

Mr Webster showed Inspector Brunt to the door.

In the dinner-hour, while we were eating our slabs of cold suet pudding on an old bench in the yard, we came in for a lot of teasing, some of it less than good-natured.

'It's you Hollinsheads he came for. I saw him looking at you.'

'He was up at your place in the middle of the night.'

News travelled miraculously across the empty limestone hills.

'My Dad knows Brunt. He says once he's got his teeth in you, he'll have you if it takes him twenty years.'

'He'll be waiting for you after school.'

We gave nothing away. In any case, wasn't I the only one who knew that Mr Fred had been involved? Apart from that, there was one Hollinshead commandment writ larger than the rest: we never spoke of family business outside the house, whatever the provocation. We learned that rule while we were still being taught to walk.

Lilian took our class during the afternoon. Whenever that happened, we became a living proof of our tribal solidarity. We could make Lilian's life misery at home, especially when she was sitting at the kitchen table, trying to study in the evening. Looking back, I know that she worked hard—but she also knew how to shelter behind her books when there were household jobs to be avoided.

In front of strangers we could behave like saints, but this afternoon was different—and I cannot blame it all on Inspector Brunt. Today's was an object lesson on *The Squirrel* and Lilian set on the table a miserable stuffed animal that came out of the cupboard once a year. It was a moth-eaten creature with one glass eye missing. She did her best to keep the empty socket turned away from us. It had an empty nutshell in its wired-up paws and its lips were curled back from its needle-like teeth in a ridiculous sneer.

I was the first to laugh, and that set off the others. If Lilian had been less conscious of her dignity, she would have laughed herself, and we would have been hers to command again within seconds. But she fell back on her artificial authority—leaving herself with no other ally but the squirrel itself. So now we were laughing at both of them. And at any minute Mr Webster, at the moment visiting the infants, would be in to investigate the noise.

'Katherine Hollinshead—I shall send you to the Desk.'

She never would! The Desk was the symbol of Mr Webster at his most terrible: the corner where one waited, the cold sweat clammy down one's spine, for him to look up enquiringly from whatever he was writing, then reach theatrically down into the knee-hole behind his wastepaper basket.

I sobered at once. The class recognized her mood and came to heel. She began to lecture us about hibernation. We had had the lesson before. We had it every year. There was comfort in the ritual. We were not going to be assailed by unfamiliar questions. I was now struggling to be good, but I suddenly caught sight of that comic animal again and started sniggering.

Lilian rapped on her table with a heavy ruler. It was an involuntary movement, a danger warning not to be ignored. She looked at the door through which Mr Webster could appear at any instant. For the second time I took fierce control of myself.

Resentment was now added to my turmoil. Would she really have sent me to Mr Webster? Our Lilian? Betray one of the family to an outsider? I tried to protect myself from another lapse by deliberately losing track of the lesson, trying not even to hear her voice: and especially not to catch sight of that ludicrous animal. Surely she would have the sense to ignore me from now on.

'So what does it remind you of? Katherine Hollinshead—I'm asking *you*.'

She had got to families of animals, wanted me to lead her to the subject of rodents in general. Some devil took charge of my tongue.

'John Palmer,' I said.

Lilian blushed. I felt as if the fire in her cheeks was reaching me where I sat. What I had just said was outrageous beyond redemption: talk of innermost secrets! Our brother Stanley saved the surface of the situation. He put up his hand.

'Please, Miss, it has teeth that go on growing when they wear away.'

This calmed her down, and she and I did what we ought to have been doing for the last five minutes—we ignored each other's existence. At four o'clock Mr Webster called me aside as the others were milling into the cloakroom. There was a hurtful gravity in his blue eyes and at first I was stupid enough to wonder what new offence could have come to light. It did not occur to me that Lilian would have reported me.

'Mutiny and rudeness to those set over us are always serious matters, Katherine. But when the one in authority is a hard-working member of your own family—'

His eyes were looking deep into my heart. You could not have secrets from Mr Webster.

'Your sister Lilian has every chance of winning her scholarship. She can win her way to college. Must I tell the Committee that her own kith and kin make it impossible for her to pursue her studies here?'

My eyes were smarting. He need have said and done no more. But after looking at me for a few more seconds, he bent towards that knee-hole, came up with his terrible crook-handled cane and straightened it out.

My body tingled as I held out my hand. I must have been a slight and trembling figure in my dress of coarse black stuff and my white creased pinafore. Mr Webster was a deeply thoughtful and kindly man, which made my shame the worse. There was a sort of kindness in his eyes as he adjusted my fingers to the angle at which he wanted them. He was not the sort of man, I tried to tell myself, who would hurt a girl more than she could stand. But he made that cane sting. And when I held out my other hand, he signed to me that he wanted the first one again, brought the cane down exactly over the first weal. Every nerve in my system quivered; and that was not because of the pain.

Then, making me hold the pen in fingers too painful to grasp it, he set me to write out three times in my best copybook hand:

As the crackling of thorns under a pot, so is the laughter of a fool.

For once, I hated coming out of the school building. The outside world was alien to me. I had violated its natural laws—and my troubles were only just beginning. When Lilian told at home of my behaviour, I could not expect easy forgiveness. So I did not hurry along the road out of Waterlow village. The Wardles and the Ollerenshaws had long since disappeared over their own horizons. I climbed the drystone wall and began my slow walk up the deserted Dumble.

Deserted? Was that sterile cleft in the hillside ever deserted? It may have been the effect of years of Lilian's stories, or simply my own scatterbrained fancies, but in that apology for a valley, I was never alone without feeling afraid. Everywhere were rocks and pinnacles, hollows and depressions from which hidden eyes could be watching me. And I was always certain that they were.

But today they were not Lilian's ghosts, in which I did not believe, nor my own, in which I did not know whether to believe or not. What I feared now was an encounter with Inspector Brunt. He must surely be waiting to waylay me in some such remote spot as this, for he had looked at me more than twice today in the schoolroom.

Like Mr Webster's, his eyes could penetrate. He must know that there was something that I could tell him. And I was even more afraid of myself than I was of him. I knew that once he started talking to me, whether it was with mock kindness or real cruelty, I must surely blurt it out sooner or later: Mr Fred. I would be forced to say it, simply because I was trying so hard not to. Was I not the only one who knew about Mr Fred, except for my mother and father?

There was an isolated, impoverished tree, growing alone on the skyline of the Dumble, and I fixed my eye on it as might a mariner on a star. At least, I would not look back over my shoulder. If Inspector Brunt were obliquely behind me, at least I would save myself from seeing him.

And there was someone waiting for me at the head of the clough; but it was not Inspector Brunt. It was Lilian, her apron ribbons fluttering in the wind.

'It won't help you to dawdle, you disgusting little bitch.'

It was a word that we were not allowed to say. She was flushed again, but not as she had been in the classroom. This was inexpressible hatred.

'I haven't told them. I've had all I can bear today, without another scene. I've told them you stayed to help Miss Hargreaves paste pictures on cards. And if ever again, you little beast—'

'I'm sorry, Lilian.'

'Sorry? What can *sorry* mean?'

It suddenly came to me why she had not given me away. If my father had discovered that she had called on the headmaster to settle a score with a sister, the echoes would have been awakened in the Dumble. Unjustly, I was saved. But Lilian was not going to let us be reconciled. She walked ahead of me, unwilling even to cross over the threshold with me.

'Lilian—'

'Don't Lilian me.'

'There was someone in the house last night.'

'Why don't you climb that tree and shout it over the hills, you young fool?'

'I know who it was.'

And this did make her slow down her pace.

'How can you know who it was?'

I was not going to tell her about the pipe tobacco. I wanted it to seem more magic than that.

'Well, go on, then — who was it?'

'Mr Fred.'

'How could it possibly have been? And how could you possibly know?'

'I am telling you —'

'Why should Mr Fred have to hide? Least of all from Inspector Brunt?'

'I am telling you —'

'You're a she-devil, Kathy. You say things that could get all manner of people into trouble. Well, here's one piece of advice for you, free and for nothing: you don't know that anyone was hiding here last night. And you don't mention Mr Fred to a soul — not even to Mother and Father.'

And then we both saw someone who had us racing each other towards the house.

CHAPTER 3

So who was Mr Fred?

At this time, when he was about to become the biggest thing in our lives, I really knew next to nothing about him. He was our father's friend, a figure from some unknown phase in his previous existence — before we were born: which means at a time that meant nothing to us.

Even now, the year before my birth seems as distant from me as Ancient Rome.

Everybody loved Mr Fred. We loved his irregular (and always unexpected) visits. He told us stories, not out of books, but real ones, about when he and my father had been young men, hiring themselves out as loaders and beaters when the big shooting-parties were up from London. He told us how my father had once allowed himself to be bribed for sixpence by a man who claimed to hypnotize the public in a booth at a village fair. But it was a fake, and my father gave the game away by doing all the wrong things on the stage: so he had his ears boxed behind the tent afterwards. It was hard to think of him ever doing anything like that. But when Mr Fred was sitting in the other corner of the hearth, even my father started telling stories. Mr Fred would take out his pocket knife and carve a spinning top out of a cotton reel. Then my father would carve one too. But he never carved anything when Mr Fred was not there.

People behaved differently when Mr Fred was about. We were never in trouble when he was about the house. Nobody lost their temper with us. The only squabble might be over who should sit next to him. I usually won.

He was different from my father: cleaner shaven, taller, burlier, softer spoken; and more given to speech. He always had sweets for us in his pocket, invariably linseed, liquorice and chlorodyne. If someone gave me a cough lozenge to suck now, I would think I was with Mr Fred. Most of all we liked to go walking with him across the fields, skirmishing to be the one to hold his hand. He would show us an ant dragging a caterpillar twenty times its size, a spider spinning its thread round the legs of a wasp. There was something about Mr Fred that people respected, and they wanted him to respect them too. Once, when Stanley and I had not set eyes on one another for some years, we met at a funeral and talked about the old days. All such conversations came round to Mr Fred.

'I was only about five or six,' Stanley said, 'And I remember hearing things that I was not meant to listen to. Dad and Mr Fred were behind the woodpile and Dad was showing him some moleskins that he had pegged out. But Mr Fred wasn't interested. He started shouting at dad, threatening to thrash him with an ashplant. I don't know how I came to think so, but I was certain it had to do with Mother.'

How much do we ever know about our parents? Do I write about our father as if we did not love him? Of course we children loved him. No other thought could have crossed our minds. To honour our father and mother was a law not to be questioned. And we knew nothing about any other father, whose attitudes we could have compared. As a young woman, when I fell in love myself, I sometimes wondered how my mother could have loved him. And if she didn't, at what stage had she stopped loving him? Or had she in fact never stopped? Was hers that kind of love that went on loving, whatever happened?

I must be fair to my father. Kiln Farm gave him no grounds for merrymaking. Except for one field, the grazing was only fit for sheep. One of my brother William's morning tasks was an eight-mile walk with two cans of milk yoked to his shoulders. He sold from door to door, and if two customers each bought a pint short, then we were making less than the rent. In those days, cattle were not slaughtered for foot and mouth disease. My father had to go on feeding them without their yield. A bad harvest from our only mowing field meant buying hay—or reducing stock. A ewe found stiff in a snowdrift meant that someone had to wait for new boots. A hole in a henhouse floor let in the fox: the loss of two dozen birds, ten dozen eggs in a good month. William was never paid a penny in wages for a life without holidays or even

Sabbaths. No growing son of a tenant farmer in our fold of hills expected to be. If William ever had a few pennies in his pocket, they came from some odd job he had found to do for a villager. He kept an old sack in which he saved the bones of any old sheep that had died on the hills; a rag-and-bone man gave him sixpence for what it took him three years to collect. The highest my father ever rose was to make ends meet. He clung desperately to his principles and his pride. They were all he had, and they cost him nothing. Other people paid that price.

It was as a result of all this—and because of a sort of accident—that my mother developed a sideline of her own, in which we older girls were expected—indeed often delighted—to help. An unnamed gentleman with a taste for rough country was walking the hills, caught in a sudden storm and came into our yard for shelter. He said something about his kingdom for a cup of tea, and this put an idea into my mother's head. She cleaned out a shed, put in a deal table and whitewashed the walls. Then she hung a board on the gate proclaiming

POT'S OF TEA.

I remember Lilian taking her to task for that apostrophe. My mother rounded on her. It was not for a child to 'take up' an elder. I am ashamed to admit that I was delighted to see Lilian in disgrace. We were always venomously jealous of each other.

It did not stop at pots of tea. My mother scraped up enough to buy a crate of stone-ginger beer and at holiday weekends she would do a special batch of baking. She had a way with pastry that she did not succeed in teaching to any of us girls.

Some wanderers came regularly. And late on that afternoon when Lilian had had me caned, it was the sight of two of our frequent customers coming up the hill that had us running home to serve them. One of them was a good-looking young fellow of seventeen or eighteen whose father was an auctioneer, and who lived in one of the better-class houses on the edge of Chapel-en-le-Frith: John Palmer. Lilian was blushfully in love with him, and it was not only for cakes and ginger beer that he came up here. It goes without saying that he did not look at all like a stuffed squirrel.

My mother came out with the teapot and cakes and signalled to me to go into the house. Sometimes she allowed us to stay and talk to our visitors, sometimes not. She was normally not keen on allowing Lilian to loiter with John Palmer, but today she seemed to be overlooking it.

As soon as I got into the kitchen, I saw that something unusual was happening. My father had his hat on and none of the other children were in the room. Some excuse had been thought of to get them out of the way.

'Don't stand there pouting. I've a job for you.'

I often thought that my mother was harder on me than on any of the others. There were some tasks that seemed to come to me more often than was my share: scrubbing out the dairy, for example. I once heard her tell a great-aunt that I was the only one who had never had to be sent to do it again.

But it was not the dairy today. There were two baskets on the table, one a shopping-basket, packed full, with a tea-towel laid over it. The other was the square one in which my father carried his lunch when he was working far from the house.

'Take this basket. Go down the Dumble and up the track to the old limekiln. Set it down just inside the arch and come straight home again. Don't loiter. If anyone asks you where you're going, say that old Granny Smailes has been ill with bronchitis and that I've sent you with a bowl of broth and a hambone for her.'

That was all the explanation I was given. In those days it was believed that the less children knew, the less they had to worry about; and the less they might give away. I picked up the basket. I knew it was for Mr Fred.

'Not yet,' my mother said, short with me because her nerves were on edge. 'Your father will give a call.'

He went out, taking his own basket. I asked no questions; they would have been snapped aside. Five minutes later we heard the plaint of a lapwing some quarter of a mile away. My father was good at bird calls; he had learned them when he and Mr Fred were young men.

'Now!' my mother said. 'Get back as soon as you can, and don't tell any of the others where you've been.'

I headed for the Dumble: twisted rock sentinels and an evening chill whispering through the nettlebeds. Another half-hour and the sun would be below the hills. There was a feeling of autumn in the valley and I walked quickly. I knew that Mr Fred was lying low somewhere about the farm, perhaps in the dilapidated old kiln itself, and I pictured it—my imagination must have been in fine fettle—turned into a snug little home for a man in hiding.

I had to leave the clough bottom and climb a steep flank round a knob of exposed rock. The Dumble was an eerie place, but whatever shivers it gave me, I saw no reason to be afraid of Mr Fred. As I passed, a jackdaw proclaimed his territorial rights over an old quarry-face. We had nursed a jackdaw in the house for some time, when he had been found with his leg broken in a trap: Jacob. I tried to believe that this bird was Jacob, and that he remembered me.

The kiln was not very far now. I began to walk more slowly, hoping that Mr Fred would come out of hiding. I badly wanted to see him. Somewhere, not a stone's throw away, he must be waiting; watching perhaps from within the fire-arch of the kiln itself, or lying flat behind a lip of ground. He would see me coming and as soon as he was

sure I was not being followed, he would come out to meet
me.

I began to walk more slowly, but Mr Fred did not
appear. There was no sign about the mouth of the kiln
that it could possibly be inhabited. It was partially
choked with rubble and rubbish. I hated the thought of
putting my basket down. I hated to turn my back and
walk away without having seen Mr Fred. I stood and
looked round the fading green and rock-scarred bowl of
land. A ewe, browsing on a ledge, raised her head and
looked casually down at me. In the middle distance a
hawk was hovering over prey invisible to me. Behind me
Jacob—if it was Jacob—was still making a fuss.

Then I heard Mr Fred coming, and it was not out of
the kiln that he came. He might sleep in there at night,
but it would be madness to spend his day within closed
walls. It would be like waiting inside a trap of his own
choosing. He would be up among the crags somewhere,
keeping his eye on the approaches. And it was from just
such a vantage point that I heard him coming now: a
slither of loose stones under his feet: an unevenness of
steps. *Left, right, slither, left, left, right*—and then a
little jump. I turned to look in the direction of the sound.
A man sprang down on to the turf less than thirty yards
from me.

But it wasn't Mr Fred. It was Inspector Brunt.

CHAPTER 4

I have never known for certain what went wrong. My
father must have given his lapwing call the moment he
felt certain that Inspector Brunt had picked up his trail:
that was why he had gone out carrying his basket—as a
decoy. And when it came to leading a stranger on a wild-

goose chase through these hills, there could be no equal to my father. Except Mr Fred.

But perhaps Inspector Brunt had also seen John Palmer and his friend leave the farm. He might have fallen back to pay attention to them — and then caught sight of me. Perhaps he had even guessed from the beginning what my father was up to.

I waited five agonizing seconds as he came and took my basket from my hand. I had no silly thought of trying to run away. The hideousness of the man held me frozen: his lumpy face and his pale-looking eyes with their painful red rims. The cold of the evening was making them water, and he had to keep dabbing them with his handkerchief.

'A heavy basket for a little girl a long way from home. You've come to feed the crows, perhaps?'

Perhaps he did not know a crow from a jackdaw.

'I'm taking this to Granny Smailes. She's been ill with bronchitis. My mother has sent her some food.'

'Your mother often sends you out like this, does she — alone in the failing light?'

'Only because Granny Smailes has been ill.'

Inspector Brunt looked significantly at the kiln.

'What do they call you, child?'

'Kathy, sir.'

'That's an old limekiln, isn't it, Kathy? Let's have a look at it, shall we?'

I was never more frightened in my life than as we came under the shadow of that ugly arch. I was frightened for Mr Fred's sake and for my own. I was convinced that Inspector Brunt could lock me up for helping Mr Fred. I might never see my parents or Kiln Farm again. And I was frightened too of what we might see when we did go into the kiln. The kiln was that sort of place. You could not see where the inside darkness led to. There was something cruel in the shape of its mouth, something heathenish about its crumbling walls: the place had been in disuse for years. It smelled bad. The clean-picked skull of a rat lay against a fallen coping-stone.

'Aren't you afraid?' Inspector Brunt asked, making his voice sound friendly and gentle.

'No, sir.'

'Good girl. There's nothing to be afraid of, is there?'

'No, sir.'

He moved a pace ahead of me and peered into the kiln.

'You might as well come out, Needham!'

The arch threw back an empty echo. My insides shrank at the way the Inspector called Mr Fred just by his second name.

No reply came out of the kiln. Inspector Brunt brought a slip of paper out of his pocket, folded it into a spill and lit it with a match. Sheltering it from draughts behind his cupped palm, he ducked under the roof and scrambled over the rubble into the darkness. It was clear that there was no one in there but he looked hard into every corner. Twice he stooped to pick something up. I could not see what he had found.

Then he came out again, took me by the hand, and I was surprised how dry, firm and cool his fingers were.

'So: Granny Smailes. We must not keep her waiting for her supper, must we?'

'No, sir.'

'It seems a funny place for your Granny to live, up here.'

'Sir, she isn't really my Granny. We only call her that. Because she's old. This is a short cut.'

I was glad that this was true, otherwise Inspector Brunt would have been asking more sharp questions.

'I'll come with you,' he said. 'It will be nice for you to have company, won't it?'

I did not answer at first so he repeated the question, not unkindly, but with enough insistence to show that silence could not help me.

'Won't it, Kathy?'

'Yes, sir.'

'I don't believe you really think so. I don't believe you like me. Now I wonder why that is? Don't you know that policemen are always nice to good people?'

'We have to turn off here,' I said.

It was a gap in a wall. Inspector Brunt got his coat caught as he tried to get through.

'I'm afraid we made a lot of noise in your house last night, Kathy. Not too long before you went to sleep again, I hope? I'm sorry I snatched your bedroom door open like I did. Had you been standing there long?'

'Not long, sir.'

'How long?'

'Not very long.'

'Come along, Kathy. That's no sort of answer. How long?'

'Just a few minutes, sir.'

'So what did you see? What made you get out of bed in the first place?'

'Sir, all the noise down in the yard.'

'That was my fault. I'm sorry. But you couldn't see the yard through your keyhole, could you? What *did* you see?'

'Sir, I saw my mother come out of her bedroom.'

'Your mother? And your father—where was he?'

'Sir, he was in bed.'

'You're sure of that. It didn't take him very long to come downstairs afterwards, did it? Was he in bed fully dressed?'

'Sir, he was in his nightshirt.'

'Do you often see your father in his nightshirt?'

'Not often, sir.'

'But you're sure it was your father that you saw last night?'

Sir, who else could it have been?

But at that age my wits were not fast enough for such
an ideal answer. I could only repeat what I had said,
mumbling, which I knew would show that I was worried.
But Inspector Brunt did not give me time to think.

'And what did your mother do, Kathy? Did she go
straight downstairs? Did she go straight and open the
kitchen door?'

I was tempted then to tell a bare-faced lie. But I
suppose that I wanted to stay as near to the truth as
possible. When you have been taught that it is wrong to
tell a lie, you are often bad at doing it. I hesitated: and he
noticed.

'She was a long time opening the door,' I said. 'The
bolts are stiff.'

'They are, are they?'

'You have to be very strong to get them to move, sir.'

'Within the last five minutes, you have told me
something that isn't true, Kathy.'

What could I have possibly replied to that?

'You know what I am talking about, don't you?'

'No, sir.'

I was in a tangle. I had said several things that were not
true, but I did not know which one he meant.

'Just think, Kathy.'

'I can't think, sir.'

'Then we shall have to go over it all again, shan't we?'

But now we were in sight of Granny Smailes's
cottage—or, rather, her hovel. It was one of a small
hamlet—to be more accurate, of what used to be a
hamlet, for every dwelling except hers was now in ruins.
It lay in a depression where a bridle-path crossed a cart-
track.

Granny Smailes was a shepherd's widow. Many a
landlord would have had her in the poorhouse, but my
father had let her stay. It was ten years since he had been
able to pay a shepherd. He and William had to take the

sheep in their stride, along with everything else.

We children had decided that Granny Smailes was a witch. For once, this was not one of Lilian's inventions. I rather fancy that it was mine. Granny Smailes was terrifying. She had no sense of humour, no patience with anything new. Moreover, she was stone deaf. You had to shout within inches of her good ear, and quite often she would lose her temper over something that she only thought you'd said. And here was I, about to offer her a basket of food that she knew nothing about, to help her get over an illness that she had not had. It would be bad enough even trying to remind her who I was. I would have to say everything three times, and even then she would not understand. I could imagine her flinging the basket sky-high, or kicking it in fury down the garden path: all to the fascination of Inspector Brunt.

And Inspector Brunt made matters worse by sending me alone up the path while he waited behind a bulge in the wall. Thus, though he would be able to hear all we said, Granny Smailes would not know that he was there. And I could hardly shout at the top of my voice, *Don't say anything, Granny. Just take this basket off me and say thank you as if you've been expecting it. There's a detective-policeman with a face like a cold suet dumpling hiding under your wall.*

I walked alone along Granny Smailes's stone-slab path. She had not tried to do anything to her scrawny garden for years. Her bed of mint had spread everywhere. A self-sown elder had taken root in the middle of a gooseberry bush. I tapped on her door, hoping for an instant that it would be impossible to make her hear. Perhaps then I could set my basket down on her doorstep and shout, *Granny, my mother's sent this food for you. I can't stay now. I've got to get back home.*

But then Inspector Brunt would come up to the door himself and make her open it. I knocked again, forced courage on myself and really hammered. I heard footsteps inside. I heard bolts drawn.

She stood there looking at me, a little woman, a shawl about her shoulders, snuff stains down the upper part of her clothing.

'There's no need to break the door down.'

And then I knew that everything was going to be all right, because she coughed, uncontrollably, racking her body. She was a woman getting over a bad attack of bronchitis. Through wisps of hair her black eyes scanned me. I had a feeling that I had never had about Granny Smailes before: that behind those eyes there lay a knife-sharp brain.

'Which of Will Hollinshead's brood are you, then?'

'They call me Kathy.'

'You're Kathy, are you?'

She took the basket from me, turned and carried it into her house. I wished her good night and turned towards the gate. I wanted to get away before either of us had to speak again. But she knew better.

'Kathy—aren't you going to take yesterday's bowl and plates back? Has your mother enough crocks to last her a week?'

I followed her into the dingy cottage, which smelled so unwholesome that I held my breath. She unpacked my basket on to her table, put into it two empty dishes and an old pudding basin, then relaid the tea-towel over the top. I tried to peep out of the window, but could see no sign of Inspector Brunt. That was a pity: he should be seeing this. Granny Smailes came to her door with me.

'Tell your mother there's no need to send any more after today. I'll thank her myself when I see her.'

She coughed alarmingly.

Was it a miracle of putting two and two together? At the risk of spoiling a satisfying story, I must admit that there was more than one way in which Granny Smailes might have been prepared for this encounter. My father might have dropped in to see her. He might have sent William. It was even possible that Mr Fred had paid her a call.

I don't know. Nobody thought of telling me. It was better that way. Nobody, not even Inspector Brunt, could force out of me what I had not been told. But I was twelve — and I still wanted to believe in magic. I think I would rather never know the truth behind the wisdom of Granny Smailes. I would like to go on thinking that it was wisdom.

CHAPTER 5

When we were a little way down the hill, Inspector Brunt unpacked my basket, turned over in his hands the bowls and dishes that the old woman had put in there. They were her own: chipped at the edges, with a network of hairline cracks under the glaze, choked with black grime. Our home was poor, but my mother kept it extraordinarily decent. Mr Brunt must have know that she would never have owned such crockery. But he did not say anything. In fact he started talking about things that did not seem to matter.

'I saw you in the schoolroom this morning, Kathy.'

'I know, sir.'

'Your big sister teaches in the school, doesn't she?'

'Yes, sir.'

'Doesn't that make it a little awkward sometimes?'

'Not really, sir.'

'Does she try to boss you about at home sometimes?'

I did not reply to this. I resented it. I was very conscious of what belonged to Inspector Brunt and what belonged to us Hollinsheads. At one point he dropped my hand and slid his fingers over my shoulder. I cringed away.

'What's the matter, Kathy? You're not ticklish, are you?'

'I don't know, sir.'

A silly answer; but he took his hand away and did not touch me again.

'Do your brothers and sisters often tickle you?'

'No, sir.'

'And Fred Needham? What do you call Fred Needham?'

'Mr Fred, sir.'

'Does Mr Fred sometimes tickle you?'

'No, sir.'

I could not remember that he ever had. And in any case, what did it matter?

'When did you last see Mr Fred, Kathy?'

'Oh, it was a long time ago—a very long time.'

'I see. And have you ever been alone with him, Kathy—just you and Mr Fred in the room?'

'I can't remember.'

'And you can't remember whether he ever tried to put his arm round you, or tickle you, or anything?'

'No, sir.'

He brought me to the farmyard gate and I expected him to come into the house with me. But he handed me my basket and turned away down the Dumble.

My father was home again, furious that a child had been questioned in this way. Inspector Brunt was a brute, a bully and a trouble-stirrer. I had to repeat my conversation with him three times, and then it was I who became the butt of my father's rage. I was not to be trusted. I was a little fool who talked too much. Why had I said that about seeing him in bed? Why had I told Brunt about my mother's struggle with the bolts? Lilian, sitting at the table with a map of the northern hemisphere, always ready to be the martyr of people's noisy talk when she had a book open, looked at me as if she thought I was the last person who ought to have been sent on a tricky errand. My mother, standing near the window, suddenly raised a hand for silence.

'I thought I heard someone.'

'I wouldn't put it past that clinker-faced jack o' lantern to be listening under the eaves.'

With a threatening scowl, my father went out of the house.

'You haven't had your supper yet,' my mother said, and put on the table a plate of cold rabbit-pie, a hand-chosen helping, with a corner-piece of pastry soaked in gravy. Lilian shifted her atlas a bad-tempered inch away from me. My mother sent her upstairs to see if baby Thomas was awake, thus leaving herself alone in the room with me.

'Kathy: when you were peeping from your bedroom door—what *did* you see?'

'Nothing,' I said. I wanted to be rid of the whole burden. For a second I thought she would chide me for refusing to be helpful. But no such idea seemed to strike her.

'Nothing,' she said. 'That's what it's always best to have seen and heard.'

A few minutes later, my father came in again, having made the immediate round of the house and yard without finding anyone.

Lilian did not tell us any ghost stories tonight. The day had been enough, without having to call on imaginary horrors. I knew also that she was piqued because I knew something more than she did about what was going on; she was dying to attack me with a string of questions. However strained things were between us in the daytime, we often found ourselves talking amicably once we were under the sheets and the candles were out.

But tonight Lilian did not begin a conversation.

Obviously she did not want to put unnecessary ideas into the younger ones' heads. But their ears, it seemed, had been doing their own foraging.

Lilian had turned her back to me and when, in search of friendship, I tried to touch the calf of her leg with my foot, she drew it sharply away from me. Then Emily, aged eight, threw her bombshell.

'Why didn't Mr Fred wait till we came home from school?' she asked.

And Lilian then made one of her typical mistakes. She pounced on Emily for knowing anything at all about Mr Fred, told her not to talk such stupid nonsense, demanded to know what had put such a ridiculous notion into her head. She made it sound as if it was an act of wickedness to have stumbled on to a piece of news. I knew what would happen—Emily was a stubborn child. It would be impossible to get information out of her now. Lilian began to relent and tried to wheedle her.

'Whatever has made you start thinking of Mr Fred, of all people?'

'I shan't tell you.'

Emily was like that. Her snivelling could go on late into the night.

'Mr Fred indeed! When did any of us last see Mr Fred?'

'Tell us a story, Lilian,' I said, to take Emily's mind off the subject.

'No.'

It was going to be that sort of night. But then we heard the house door open and somebody went out across the yard: my father, obviously. He must be going out to see Mr Fred, out there where the night would be long, dark, damp and cold. I felt Lilian's body stiffen next to mine as, like me, she strove to identify each sound. Emily's snuffling reached a convulsive crisis.

'Shut up!' Lilian said.

We heard Brindle pull at her chain and start to

whimper at the notion of an outing. My father unfastened her. The hinges of the gate creaked; we heard him deal with the catch. Then he was gone, and there was no sound in the night other than the wind in the trees and a petty flurry in the poultry-shed as something disturbed the hens: a rat, perhaps, in the earth under their roost.

I listened for other sounds until the silence itself was pounding my eardrums like a tide. Out there, Inspector Brunt was probably still lurking. And if my father were to walk into a trap, that was not something that would peter out in a handful of artful questions. Inspector Brunt would not deal with my father as gently as he had dealt with me. I loved my father; at least, if you had asked me at this time, I would have protested that I did. True, I feared his every threat and movement; we all did. Not one of us drew ourselves to his attention more than we absolutely had to. But I could not bear the thought that anything might happen to him. There was comfort in what was familiar.

So I resolved not to go to sleep until I heard him return. I listened, trying to isolate any out-of-the-ordinary sound that might tell me something. But the night was like an unremitting surf, broken only by the taps, rustles and jingles of the deserted yard. A broken length of downpipe swung on its guttering. A cat upset a pile of rubbish. Something rattled against a sheet of loose iron. Soon I was the only one in the room who was awake. Even Lilian, for all her earlier curiosity, was breathing softly and regularly.

The last time I heard the clock downstairs, it struck three. The small hours were long ones. When getting-up time came, I had had very little rest. But I had to face the cruel, chilly morning. And what was especially cruel was that my father had not come home by breakfast-time.

CHAPTER 6

How much do we know about our parents? Are they real to us at all? How much did I know about my parents when I was twelve?

I knew that my mother could be frighteningly strict about moral and personal things. Now, with a lifetime's experience behind me, I know that she was not given to revealing her feelings. We never doubted her love, but it was not her way to show herself warmly loving. I think she knew a lot more about what went on in our childish minds than she ever let us see. She had been—no, that is unjust—she *was* a proud woman. Before she married, she had been in service in a wealthy household. She spoke little of it, but when she did, it was as if she had held a position of dignity and distinction. She must at one time have had ambitions, and I have always assumed that these were rooted in the things she admired about the family she had served. Kiln Farm must have been the crushing of those ambitions; and yet, somehow, in a manner that grew colder as the years passed, her dignity remained.

I have two portraits of her. In one she is with her parents: a bearded father of the country working-class, and a tight-haired, tight-lipped, tight-stayed mother in severe black satin. My mother is sitting on a stool at their feet, an only child—at least, she was at the age of three. She has a white bow in her hair, and her cheeks are scrubbed to a shine. She looks very solemn. All three of them do. I never met my grandparents, or indeed any members of my mother's family. Sooner or later, I guessed that there had been an estrangement. I did not easily discover what it had been about.

The second portrait is a silhouette made when she was about twenty: a likeness reduced from a shadow on a screen, as was fashionable in the last century. My mother had a high bosom and a high-piled, precarious hair-style. I have often found it quite remarkable how children can form astute ideas on forgotten evidence, and I always knew that that silhouette had something to do with excursions in the hills when my father and Mr Fred were reckless young gallants.

Of my father I knew a good deal less. He was the undisputed master of everything we did; more than that we did not need to know about him. I never heard my mother question his judgement or decrees; if she ever did so within her heart, that was something that she kept from us. She never talked to us about him. The only one who ever did that was Mr Fred. And all we ever heard from him was of a lively young man playing irresponsible pranks about the countryside. We believed those tales, because Mr Fred told them, but the reality behind them was hard to accept.

It was a frightening morning when my father, having to the best of my belief been out all night, did not appear at the breakfast-table. I was worried sick, yet I dared not ask a question. I looked round the room for any information that might be gained. The shopping-basket that I had carried was still in its place; but my father's lunch-box was missing.

At ten minutes past eight, he came in across the yard, glancing at the plates on the table, the time by the mantel clock, Stanley cleaning Emily's boots for her. There was nothing with which he could immediately find fault—but then, some mornings, there did not need to be. He could whip himself into a passion over nothing, and we would stand meekly through it, silent round the table. We would not have dared a word in self-justification. It is sometimes said that more than anything else, children

resent injustice. We didn't. Nobody had talked to us
about justice.

But this morning he found nothing out of order. My
mother came over from the range with oatcakes fried in
home-cured bacon fat. My father stood behind his
uncushioned wooden chair and nominated Emily to say
Grace. She did so simply and clearly; as a matter of habit,
he told her not to mumble. We stood and ate in heavy-
breathing silence. As we left the house, my mother held
Stanley back to reinforce a loose thread on a tunic
button. He soon caught us up, and there was nothing
unusual in our strung-out descent of the Dumble — except
that Stanley and Emily seemed to have developed an
unprecedented preference for each other's company.
Dear Stanley: even at that age the most lively and
intelligent of us — and always the most obliging to younger
and older alike. And Emily was throughout her life the
most easily impressed, the most ready to believe in
prophecies of calamity: and the least able to cope with
disaster when it happened.

Sometimes two of us would be temporarily drawn
together by sharing something — a planned practical joke,
or an item of secret knowlege. Stanley and Emily were in
one of those phases now. Something must have honed
their curiosity. That must be how Emily had come to
know about Mr Fred.

Now the pair were well behind us, talking intensely. A
late brown butterfly, mistaking the season, was clinging
to a gorse-bush, unable to open his wings for the cold.
When Stanley failed to notice it, I knew how preoccupied
he was. Lilian buttonholed me as we reached the road,
and she was beginning to whip us together into a tight
defensive bunch.

'Those two know something.'

'I know.'

'Keep an eye on them — especially at playtime and

dinner. They mustn't *say* anything.'

'They wouldn't.'

'Stanley wouldn't.'

'They'll take more notice of you than they will of me, Lilian.'

'I can't be everywhere at once, can I?'

'You think I can, then?'

The Wardles were behind us on the road, so we kept our close formation. They wouldn't risk physical assault with Lilian in the middle of us. But like a collie that could cut an individual sheep out of a flock, they knew how to isolate weaklings. We heard a scamper of feet, as if they were having a race among themselves. Lilian increased her pace and we followed suit, Caroline having to trot to keep up with us. A sharp flat stone came skimming up the roadway and caught the back of her leg. She tumbled to her knees.

Tears and screams; blood from a scratch, dust and gravel to be wiped out of it; a handkerchief to be wrapped round it. By this time, the Wardles had caught us up, seven or eight of them, and went stamping on as if they were a regiment plunging into an attack.

'Bernie Wardle, you threw that stone.'

'I didn't.'

'I saw you.'

That was Lilian not using her brains, losing the argument before it had fairly started. She could not possibly have seen him. We were a milling chaos now of Hollinsheads and Wardles. Lilian veered to a diagonal course, trying to lead us out of the tangle. But a nucleus of Wardles somehow got under her feet. It was a battle of family identities, a feud of which neither side knew the origins. Lilian side-stepped, scooping up Caroline to her shoulder. Caroline howled. The rest of us somehow contrived to stay together, so that the two families were now abreast across the middle of the road. When Lilian slackened her pace, so did the Wardles. When she tried to press ahead, they did the same. When one of them kicked a stone, it ricocheted ahead of us, like the one that had struck Caroline.

'I only stubbed my toe against it, see?'

He had his excuses ready, in case she took him up to Mr Webster. But I knew she wouldn't. After yesterday she would not lightly call on Mr Webster again. And I think the Wardles knew that too.

'They've got Fred Needham sleeping rough up at their place.'

They did not shout insults directly at us: they made loud comments about us among themselves. This made it more tempting to defend ourselves.

'That Brunt will have him. My Dad says Brunt won't care if he has to wait years.'

'Their Dad will be locked up.'

'They call it harbouring a fugitive.'

'My Dad says it isn't right for us to have to do as *she* tells us.'

'She isn't a real teacher.'

'She won't even be a pupil-teacher much longer.'

'She even gets her own sister caned.'

And then a filthy lie.

'Fred Needham's only killed half a dozen kids.'

We did not have a daily newspaper at Kiln Farm. Once a week, when he went to Chapel-en-le-Frith, my father brought home the *High Peak News*, but it contained only local items, up to a week old. I don't believe the Wardles spent money on a daily paper either—but the press was not the only source of news. It used to astonish me how much information my father used to be able to gather without leaving our own fields.

Walking along the stone-dust road to Waterlow, I rejected what the Wardles had said. It was a lying taunt. I knew that Mr Fred was keeping his head down somewhere about our property. I was prepared to accept that in some petty way he had fallen foul of the law: it was common grown-up talk that the law was capricious. I expected Lilian to speak up in Mr Fred's defence. But she didn't. She ignored the Wardles, set down Caroline and told her that she must walk.

'I can't. My leg's gone stiff.'

Stanley came to her rescue, demonstrating with his usual whimsical logic that she still possessed the ability to set one foot in front of the other. He and Caroline fell a few steps behind the rest of us, the safest place now for them to be. Within less than a minute, Caroline laughed at something Stanley said. In some ways he was a minor genius.

The school day was free from most of its embarrassing possibilities. Inspector Brunt did not appear, and Mr Webster did not put Lilian in charge of our class. In the yard Emily and I managed to stay within a protective ring of other girls—Caroline had a separate playtime with the infants' class. As long as we remained in sight of Mr Webster's window, we felt reasonably safe.

But Stanley could not surround himself with a defensive cordon of girls and I saw that a roving gang of Wardles and Ollerenshaws had managed to press him over to a corner of the coke-heap, a common assembly-point when something unsavoury was being cooked up. They had formed a half-circle round him: boys in knee-breeches, boys in corduroys, boys with their shirt-tails hanging through the seat of their trousers. And they were abusing him with questions. I could not hear what was being said, but I could see that he was standing placid and confident, his feet slightly apart, appearing to give as good as he was getting. I knew that they would not trick Stanley into giving anything away. We girls were playing hopscotch—clumsy buttoned boots straddling lines that we had scratched on the asphalt with a stone. I twice nearly lost my turn.

I could see that Stanley was holding his own; in words, at any rate. But the 'trial'—it was hardly less than that—passed the stage of verbal taunts. Bernie Wardle and Frank Ollerenshaw each picked up a lump of coke and were about to throw it at Stanley when Mr Webster's whistle blew. I was not able to question Stanley until we were back on our way up the Dumble.

'Stanley—why have you been putting silly ideas into Emily's head?'

'They're not silly ideas, Kathy. You know they're not.'

'So what do *you* know, Stanley?'

'I'll do you a swap, Kathy—for what *you* know. I know you were sent out yesterday afternoon with a basket.'

'To Granny Smailes. Because she's been ill.'

'She hasn't. And the police detective caught up with you at the kiln, and went to Granny Smailes's house with you.'

'How do you know that?'

Stanley looked as unaffected by the world as a young owl.

'Because there are corners of our house where sound carries. And don't ask me where I mean, because there isn't room for two in there.'

He meant a narrow corner-cupboard in the boys' bedroom. It stood directly over the chimney-cupboard in the kitchen.

'So you know everything that's going on?'

'Not everything. There are some things that I can't make out.'

'Such as?'

'Why all the fuss, anyway? Why did Mr Fred come in the first place? It's obviously rubbish about him being a murderer. But the police are after him for something. And where is he now?'

'Emily said something silly about him in bed last night.

About him not waiting till we got home from school.'

'She got that off me. It seems it isn't safe to tell Emily anything.'

'I'm glad you're learning.'

'I told her because it was the only way of getting her to help. I thought she might be able to dig something out of you and Lilian. Anyway, we were home first yesterday. You had been kept behind.'

'There's no need to remind me.'

'Mother wasn't in the house.'

'That's unusual.'

'She came in out of breath, as if she'd been trying to beat us to it.'

'She could have been collecting eggs.'

'In her go-to-town coat?'

'That's strange. But it doesn't prove—'

'And I smelled pipe-tobacco, too.'

'Mr Fred's. That's how I guessed.'

'And there was a spill of paper in the hearth. The sort with a little twist at the end, the way Mr Fred makes them.'

'So could anybody else. Dad uses spills.'

'But he never gives them that extra twist. I've watched him.'

'So Mr Fred must have been in the house in broad daylight. After all the trouble—'

'That's what it looks like. And something else. There was a red and white handkerchief under Dad's chair. Not one of ours. Mother snatched it up the moment she saw me looking at it.'

'It's a pity you had to blurt this out to Emily.'

'She was with me. She saw the same things herself.'

'They wouldn't mean anything to her. Emily looks at things and doesn't see them.'

'I swore her to silence.'

'We shall have to do more than that. We shall have to

scare the wits out of her—and keep her scared. I'll ask Lilian to help.'

We were home now. And today Mother was in. The smell of baking met us as we opened the door. She had made little men of left-over pastry, with currants for buttons and eyes, and horse-teeth smiles, scratched with the prongs of a fork. There was one for each of us waiting on the table.

CHAPTER 7

My mother lost no time in getting me on my own, sending me to turn the butter-churn and following me into the dairy.

'You had some nasty frights yesterday, Kathy, what with Granny Smailes and that policeman. I hope you haven't said anything to the others.'

'Lilian knows.'

'Well, of course Lilian knows. Lilian has known all along.'

'Emily knows.'

'How on earth can Emily know?'

'Stanley told her.'

'And who told Stanley?'

'He worked it out for himself.'

'How could he?'

I told her about the pipe-tobacco and the twisted spill. I said nothing about the corner-cupboard and some instinct made me suppress the red and white handkerchief.

'Well, they'll have to be untold,' my mother said. 'I'll speak to them in turn. And I want you to put it out of your mind from now on. Mr Fred has gone.'

'Gone? You mean that Inspector Brunt—?'

'No. He got away while Inspector Brunt was busy somewhere else. And we shan't be seeing him again—or, with any luck, Inspector Brunt either.'

'Mother—'

I was dreading to have to say this to her, but I could not stop myself. If I had been familiar with the word *compulsive* in those days, I would have known that that was what it was. But I found it hard to go on, even when I had made a start.

'What is it, Kathy?'

'The Wardle boys—'

'What about the Wardle boys? Have they been pushing you about again?'

'No. Not that, They've been saying—'

'What have they been saying? I insist on knowing.'

'They've been saying that Mr Fred has killed someone.'

I cannot describe my feelings after I had got the words out. My heart was beating fast, my breathing out of my control. My mother went red. She closed her eyes in a kind of weary horror.

'It isn't true, is it, Mother?'

'Of course it isn't true. Don't you know Mr Fred better than that? People say terrible things, Kathy. But ask yourself this: what can the Wardle boys possibly know about it? How can they know the first thing about Mr Fred?'

'But the Wardles do know that Mr Fred was here,' I said doggedly.

'They know a lot of things. Some people know everything—except that there are some things that they will never know.'

I did not know what she meant by that. But she went on before I could ask.

'Who heard the Wardles say this to you?'

'Stanley and Lilian. Emily and Caroline.'

'Caroline? Oh God, no!'

Then suddenly she regained her composure.

'Go back into the house, Kathy. I'll finish the butter.
It'll do me good to use up some energy. And don't talk to
the others about any of this. Leave everything to me.'

During the evening she took them aside one after the
other: Emily called into the scullery, Stanley to help with
a shutter that had come off a hinge. She would
presumably talk to Lilian after the rest of us had gone to
bed. My father played no part in these talks. He sat in his
chair, occasionally turning a page of *Pilgrim's Progress*,
the only book that he ever read, looking now and then to
see whether a coal on the fire might be blazing wastefully.
He kept a little jar of water in the hearth for damping
down flames that might have been costing us money.

So it was over. Mr Fred had gone.

We accepted the urgent need for silence. We stopped
discussing the matter with each other: even Lilian and I
in bed. Even Stanley and I on the way down and up the
Dumble. An odd thing was that the Wardles did not
bring it up again either. One or the other of them must
have let it drop at home how they had got on to us — and
had been told that that was to be the end of it. Some
things were so appalling that they had no part in ordinary
quarrels. Some peculiar — and strong — ideas prevailed in
our neighbourhood.

The autumn days darkened; we heard no more of Mr
Fred. Then we began to notice new little things. More
frequently than ever before, my father was missing when
we came down to breakfast. Once or twice he had not
even arrived when the food was on the table. With an
anxious glance at the clock, my mother called on one of
us for Grace and we started eating without him: which at
one time would have been high treason. When he came in
five minutes later, he drew up his chair without saying a
word.

Then an old wooden table was brought out from a pile

of junk in one of the sheds. It stood out in the yard, and when we came home from school we saw that it had been scrubbed. The next day it had disappeared.

Other things happened. We developed a sharp eye for details. We knew intimately, for example, the contents of our knife-drawer. There was a knife with a groove in its handle from having been left lying against the hot edge of the frying pan. There was a fork that none of us liked because it had a twisted tine. And these things simply ceased to be there. Neither my mother nor my father questioned their absence. And some hidden voice inside us told us not to comment about them. It is not surprising that we began to talk secrets among ourselves again, particularly Stanley and I. Stanley got himself into his listening cupboard again.

'They were definitely talking about Mr Fred last night. I heard Dad say that the worst was blown over now, and that he ought to be able to move on again after Christmas.'

The comings and goings of my father's lunch-basket became a fascination in themselves. Sometimes it was on the shelf, sometimes it was missing. He did not always take it with him these days on his working journeys. And sometimes when he did, he came back without it. We were now in danger of looking on the whole affair as some sort of game.

CHAPTER 8

I had other difficulties around this time—strictly troubles of my own. I find them difficult to describe, though easy to account for—now. I was constantly making trouble for myself. I found it increasingly impossible to get on with Lilian. I began to be naughty, sometimes consciously naughty, even in the classroom. And I did not feel penitent, even when Mr Webster showed his exasperation with me. (He did not ever cane me again. I would not have cared if he had. The way he chose to hurt me now was simply to behave as if I was not worthy of his attention.) I often behaved horribly to my mother.

One evening, for example, she told me to get on with a deep pile of ironing while she sat in one of the more shadowy corners and nursed a headache with her fingers spread over her temples. I had never known her behave like that before, but I felt no sympathy for her. Her misery, in fact, seemed to drive me in the opposite direction.

'Why always me?'

It was as near to open rebellion as anything I had ever known to happen in our house, but I could not stop myself. My father was not in the room. His presence was about the only thing that would have held me in check. And even as I heard my own voice, I cringed mentally in front of the explosion that must come. I seemed to walk wilfully into an explosion two or three times every day. But my mother did not explode. She simply took her hands away from her eyes and looked at me. I knew that it was without love. I knew that I deserved none.

'Get on with that ironing.'

I got up from the corner of the floor where I was sitting with my back to the wall. Actually I was doing nothing at all. I was simply indulging in private unhappiness. Lilian seemed deep in a botany book, though I knew that she was ardently listening for a family row. The younger ones were squabbling over a rag doll. Stanley was poring over a broken-spined book: he hung about very artfully when Mr Webster was cleaning out old cupboards.

I went as slowly as I dared to the ironing-board, tears brimming inside me at the unfairness of life. The stack of work to be done looked like a mountain. I hated it. As I picked up each garment, I hated the one who wore it. I began to snuffle. In the end, my mother got up from her chair, pushed me out of the way and picked up the iron herself.

It is easy to explain now: my *age*. But in the days when I was growing up, that was not a plea for tolerance. We were expected to behave normally. If we didn't, we were punished until the passage of time made us normal. If that did not work, I suppose we remained oddities.

Did I know myself that I was growing up? In a way I did. In other ways, that affected me deeply, I didn't. I knew, for example, that my breasts were beginning to grow—just, but perceptibly. And I was proud of them. Sometimes in bed I would slip my hand under my nightdress and feel at myself. Lilian, whom I had thought to be asleep, told me angrily to stop: I ought to be ashamed of myself.

I was proud of some things, but mostly I was frightened. I remember once craftily loitering on my way home from school and detaching myself from the others. I climbed a little way up the slope of the Dumble and stood under a lonely tree that had always had a sort of magically protective role in my infantile fantasies. I felt strange, and yet I could not have said what the strangeness was. I think I knew that I was at the exit from childhood. I had no idea what was going to happen to me, but I could not stand life going on the way it was.

In some inexplicable way the distress and disarray of growing up were entangled with Mr Fred. I dreamed about his smiling face and his strong outdoor frame. In the years immediately after the First World War, settling down with a husband who encouraged me to be an adult, I started reading books about psychology. So I have no difficulty now in recognizing the eroticism of those dreams. But intimate relationships, as such, did not come into them. As an adolescent I knew very little of what

went on between men and women, and most of what I
thought I did know was wrong. (I knew about animals, of
course, but I transferred nothing correctly.) In my
dreams I was simply alone with Mr Fred and he was
somehow special to me, and I was special to him. I would
put my head against his tweedy chest and sink back into
the unique comfort that he could give me.

If I had been in true command of my dreams, I would
have sunk back time and again into that one. In the
workaday reality of life, I decided to go out among the
fields and rocks and find Mr Fred. I had to see him. I had
to talk to him. I had to see his face beam with pleasure, as
it had in the old days, in the company of the young
Hollinsheads.

At this range in time, I cannot do justice to my longing
for Mr Fred. I can remember feeling as I did, but I
cannot recreate that feeling. It is like looking back
through a system of diminishing lenses to a world to
which I no longer belong. I remember that I suffered. I
remember feeling inconsolable. But I cannot make myself
feel that suffering again.

I lay awake at night and could think of no way of going
out alone to find him. I wanted to take him food, or an
old woollen scarf, perhaps, to keep him warm through
the ruthless Pennine nights. I could at least enact such
things in fantasy. I pictured myself a daily visitor to some
hide-out, high up where the sheep were grazing. I could
see that broad smile light up his face at the sight of me.

But I saw no way of putting any of this into effect. Up
in those windswept hills, with all that open space about
me, I was as much a prisoner as if I were chained in a
cell—a prisoner within family walls, family codes, family
bolts and bars.

Obviously I said no word of any of this to the others.
And yet I always felt that Lilian *knew*—not, naturally,
the detail of my thoughts, but the trend of them.

Sometimes she looked at me as if she could read my mind—and was mocking me for it. She did not need to speak to twist the knife in my misery.

One evening after I had put the younger ones to bed, Lilian beckoned me with her eyes to the table at which she had her books deployed. She had so many of them open at once that her quest for knowledge looked like a frenzy. She was preparing a lesson on latitude and longitude and was drawing lines on a sheet of squared paper. She shifted this aside and showed me a newspaper cutting that she had hidden under it. My father was sitting looking morosely into the fire. My mother was making a bread poultice for a boil on the back of Stanley's neck. We were for the moment unobserved.

There was a smudgy newsprint photograph—of Mr Fred as a younger man than any of us had ever known. But it was recognizably Mr Fred, though with dark, serious eyes—no hint at all of the catlike smile that I always associated with him. It was as if the newspaper people had gone out of their way to find a photograph that made him look really sinister.

New sightings have been reported of Derbyshire farm bailiff Frederick Arthur Needham who escaped from a remand cell in Derby Prison earlier this month. Police suspect that he may be attempting to cross Nottinghamshire and Lincolnshire on his way to the coast.

Readers will recall that Needham had been charged with the murder of a number of young girls, aged between six and fourteen, whose bodies were found savagely dismembered after unmentionable assaults.

Any information leading to the apprehension of Needham will be gladly received by the Derbyshire County Constabulary.

*

I did not, of course, believe any of it and it was clear
that my parents did not believe it either. My mother had
plainly declared his innocence to me, and neither she nor
my father would be helping him if they believed any of
these allegations. But Lilian believed what the newspaper
said—because she wanted to.

'It isn't true!' I whispered.

'Have it your own way. I only hope I never meet him in
the fields.'

I could feel the fire in my cheeks. I pointed with my
finger to 'unmentionable assaults'.

'What does that mean?'

'Things you wouldn't know about.'

And then my mother was turning round from Stanley's
neck, calling me to bring her more old rag. Deftly Lilian
slid her graph-paper back over the cutting. Was there not
some way in which I could prove that Mr Fred was not
guilty of the things that were being said about him?

Yet, strangely, it was thanks to Lilian that I did find
my way to Mr Fred. And it was all because the course of
true love was faring badly between her and John Palmer.
John Palmer had come nowhere near Kiln Farm since the
hills had started rustling with rumours about us
Hollinsheads. But there was a streak of Hollinshead
determination in Lilian that decided her to confront him.

However much we fell out with each other, we could
make shameless use of each other when we needed to; and
Lilian needed me with her that afternoon. Sometimes it
surprises me that this was so—but on balance I think I
understand it. She could be high and mighty about her
studies and the importance of her position at our school,
but stripped of these, Lilian had no more personal liberty
than I had. She could hold obstinate theories—but when
it came to acting independently, she had little
confidence. She had to have moral support that

afternoon; and there was none available but mine.

Once her mind was made up, I was amazed at the fluency and lack of conscience with which she was prepared to tell downright lies. She told my mother that there was to be a magic lantern missionary lecture in the village hall on the coming Saturday night (which was true). Mr Webster thought she ought to go to it (he probably did) and as a special concession I had been allotted a ticket so that she would not have to come home alone. Moreover, Miss Hargreaves had invited us to have tea with her at her little house in Waterlow before the meeting (a brazen fabrication).

I need not tell in close detail what took place between Lilian and John Palmer. She had sent him a note demanding that he should come to meet us in a little spinney on the far side of Waterlow. If I had been John Palmer, I would have thrown that summons on the fire, but he was a young man of essential decency. He brought with him a companion of his own age: Eric Lawson—gauche and dull.

It was obvious to me from the start that Lilian was going to handle the situation without tact. Or shall I say that, child as I was, I thought that I would have managed things very differently myself? She let herself be angry from the outset, lashing out with what she thought was a caustic wit, though in effect it served only to emphasize her inferiority to him. I could see from the way he shrugged his shoulders that he had already as good as washed his hands of her.

But as a matter of form, we did take a walk off the highroad, as had been originally suggested. Lilian had sternly drilled me that I should walk behind with Eric Lawson, keeping him safely out of earshot of all the things she had rehearsed to say. But this I did not do. For one thing, it stood out plainly that Lilian's cause was already lost. And for another, I could not stand Eric

Lawson. I saw him as a conceited bore, and he did not hide the fact that he regarded me as immature and a nuisance. I really could be a very horrible child when I chose. Perhaps I did have my shrewder moments, but I was basically still a child. I really could not keep up an acceptable conversation with an eighteen-year-old like John Palmer. I wanted to impress him, but we had no common ground. My talk was infantile. I thought myself something of a comedian and tried to show off. I squirm even now when I think of some of the things with which I tried to impress them. What a hopeless quartet we were: Lilian and John Palmer by now talking to each other only through Eric Lawson; and myself trying to crack feeble twelve-year-old jokes.

'I'll ask you a riddle,' I said, trying to monopolize John Palmer's free side.

And I tried to amuse him with the old one about a bean, a bean and a half and half a bean. I even got it wrong and had to start again several times. Then I thought of a competition: who could be quickest at reciting the alphabet backwards.

It was too much for Lilian. She wheeled on me.

'Kathy, for God's sake—'

For one of us, this was strong talk.

'For God's sake go and lose yourself! Go on—get out of my sight!'

I thought at first that this was only a kind of warning, but she repeated it and there was a rage in her eyes. Never before or after have I seen such ugliness in her.

'Go on! Let's have the benefit of your back view. Don't let me see you again till it's time for the lecture.'

I was afraid at first, ashamed and reluctant to leave them. I did neither one thing nor the other, but started to lag behind. Soon there was fifty yards' distance between me and them. Then, stopping for breath, I happened to look back over my shoulder at the line of hills where Mr

Fred was keeping himself out of sight. At once I made up
my mind.

It took me a good half-hour to reach the western edges
of the Kiln Farm fields. They were deserted. At this hour
of a Saturday afternoon, they were hardly likely to be
otherwise. Peewits, a distant sheep desultorily bleating,
the wind in isolated trees: where, in which clough or
hollow of those sterile stretches, could I begin to look for
him? There could not be a square foot of ground that
Inspector Brunt and his constables had not scoured at
some time or other. And if Inspector Brunt could not find
him, what hope had I?

But something drew me towards the limekiln, perhaps
because my visit there in Inspector Brunt's company had
etched such a compelling evil on my mind. I came over
the crest and looked down on the place. There was still
that cruel, hungry look about the archway. I skirted a
clump of gorse. A baby rabbit sat up looking at me, so
unaccustomed to a human presence that he had not yet
learned to be afraid of man.

And then I saw my father. The kiln lay in a relatively
flat clearing and he was approaching from a corner of the
Steep Wood, along a course far removed from the direct
track from home. (It was not until a long time later that I
was to learn how hard he and William had worked to
deliver food about our acres: never twice in the same
place, and often a great distance away from where Mr
Fred had made himself at home. They had worked out a
kind of code to let him know where the next delivery
would be.)

I crouched down in the long grasses. For a terrifying
moment I saw my father scanning my sector of his skyline.
He did not see me. If he had, and if the deception by
Lilian and me had come to light, I do not know what
might have happened. I believed at the time that he
might kill us. Even now, I am not sure that he would not

have done.

He passed close under where I was hiding, and when he was within a few tens of yards of the kiln I saw him stop to take stock of all quarters. Then he stooped to move a few of the large stones with which the area was scattered. When he straightened himself again, I saw that he had made a low pile of them. I guessed that he had been carrying his lunch-basket hidden under his cloak. With another quick survey of every angle of approach, he started back in the direction from which he had come.

Now I had only to wait. And perhaps—

I did not know the time. I could not judge the pace at which time was passing. I wondered what might happen if I did not get back to Waterlow in time for the meeting. And I did not care. The chill of late afternoon set the sere grasses bristling. My curiosity fought a battle with my common sense. The child inside me wanted to go down and see what my father had left under those stones. The temptation, mad as it was, was very great. I fought it. And after half an hour—or it could have been an hour and a half—or ten minutes—I had my reward. I saw Mr Fred coming towards the cache as if he had just come out of the kiln.

There was no mistaking him. I had conjured up his figure in my mind so often. And yet there were things about him, familiar things, that I had forgotten. They all came back into my mind when I actually saw him. It all seemed to have to do with angles: the flat angle at which he wore his cap; the stiff angle at which he half swung, half dragged his left leg; the listing angle at which he leaned on his stick whenever he stopped to scan the landscapes that menaced him. As soon as I saw him I got to my feet and ran down. His reaction was the last I could have expected.

'Who in the blueness of blazes are you?'

The whites of his eyes were rolling as I had seen those of

a stallion do.

'You know me, Mr Fred.'

But he didn't. And I had a moment of terrible clarity. On all his visits, although he had played the merry uncle, he had never taken any of us in as individuals. It would stir no particular memory in him if I were to tell him I was Kathy. Children sometimes have flashes of understanding that go straight to the core of the matter. They see a magnification of the truth. And when the truth is hurtful, the hurt is magnified too.

'What do they call you, child?'

'I'm Kathy.'

'Kathy what?'

'Kathy Hollinshead.'

'One of Will's? You have no business here. Haven't you been told to keep away?'

'I'm sorry, Mr Fred.'

'Don't call me that.'

He bent to bring his face close to mine, and I saw how much he had changed. He had forgotten how to smile. I had never before seen him with two days' growth of stubble on his chin. His cheeks had always been as smooth and cherubic as a baby's. But now the flesh had gone from them and there were half-moon pouches under his eyes.

'I truly am sorry,' I said.

'You'll be sorry next time I see your father.'

But I barely took that in. I had been hurt, but I would not give in: the memory of the old Mr Fred was too strong. I needed to make Mr Fred remember me. I needed to make the old Mr Fred come back. I noticed something else about him, that I supposed I had always known, but had never before taken account of: that his eyebrows were so light-coloured that he seemed to have none at all.

This was the man that they said had killed little girls. It

could not be true. I realized that my teeth were chattering. I did not know how long that had been going on.

He stood leaning at his characteristic angle, resting his hip against the handle of his stick. And his eyes seemed to change as he fixed them on me. They did not exactly soften, but there was no more anger in them, instead, an intensity that held me mesmerized. And there was something else that I had never experienced before: a physical sensation in which my body was no longer mine. It was a sort of summation of all those tinglings of the flesh that had been happening from time to time over the last year. I felt the tissues creep in my incipient breasts, and in other parts an urgent heaviness.

'Kathy — don't be afraid of me.'

'I'm not, Mr Fred.'

I was. I was afraid because an inner certainty told me that this was the elemental Mr Fred, that for the moment I was special to him, as we had been special to each other in my premature erotic dreams. And I did not want him to believe that I was afraid of him. I did not want to be afraid of him. Although I was terrified, I wanted to be special to him.

'People have been saying things to you about me, haven't they, Kathy?'

'No, Mr Fred.'

I felt as if I had been disloyal to him in even *hearing* such things. He put his arm round my waist, tightly, so that I could feel the tips of his fingers in my ribs. It did not feel ticklish, in the way that Inspector Brunt had meant the word.

'You must not tell anyone that you've seen me here, you understand?'

'Yes, Mr Fred.'

He smiled at last, something of the old smile, but there was still an expression in his eyes that did not belong to him: a mixture of fatigue, perhaps, and the habit of mind that came from being hunted. He did not smell of his usual smells, either, which I suppose were a compound of his pipe, his shaving-stick, his boot-polish and the cloth of his coat. He smelled of soil and lime and sweat.

'Would you like to know a secret, Kathy?'

I nodded, obediently eager.

'Would you like to come and see where I live?'

Now my eagerness was real.

'It isn't much of a place—but I've got it cosy. You'll be surprised. But you must promise me that you'll never tell a soul—'

For the third time I nodded, this time with all the sincerity I could put into it. He pushed himself to his feet, and then a black frown came over his features. I looked where he was looking, and saw with a shock that my brother William was standing about twenty yards from us. He did not speak. He made no move to come closer.

So what would happen now? Would William betray me? No one could ever know for certain what William might do. He was not given to talking. William cared for other people's business less than anyone I have ever known. We used to laugh about him. He never seemed to have anything in his mind except what he was doing at the moment. He did not seem to bother to think about things if he did not have to.

Mr Fred's smile had gone.

'Some other time,' he said. 'We don't want him to know the secret, do we?'

'No, Mr Fred.'

He stood thoughtful for a moment, then put a hand in his pocket and fumbled about in its depths.

'Do you ever go near a shop, Kathy?'

'There's Mrs Harrison's at Waterlow. I always pass it on school days.'

'Next time you're there, buy me an ounce of *Prince of*

Wales mixture.'

Prince of Wales: that was what I had identified on the stairs, the first night he had come. He brought out five pennies and put them into my hand.

'When you've got it, come and hide it under this stone.'

He tapped a lump of limestone with the ferrule of his stick.

'Be off with you now.'

He turned to face William, who still did not move. I made away as fast as I could, making my legs carry me, as if they were someone else's, to whom I was trying to send messages. I had gone a fair way before I dared to look round, and when I did, neither of the men was in sight. There was only the undulating expanse of coarse grass, the flanks of the hillside ridged by centuries of sheep. I arrived back in Waterlow in the grey late afternoon, with no idea of whether I was late or had time to spare before the missionary meeting.

I went into Mrs Harrison's and asked for an ounce of *Prince of Wales*, feeling like a criminal, hardly able to make the words come out of my mouth. It was not unusual for me to buy tobacco for my father in that shop: but he always smoked thin twist. Mrs Harrison, fat, wheezy, with narrow, steel-rimmed spectacles, got laboriously up from the chair on which she always sat behind her counter and reached for her jar. She said nothing, but I felt as if her eyes were accusing me.

For days I transferred that packet of tobacco from one hiding place to another. It could not have worried me more if I had stolen a golden sovereign. I could not think how I was ever going to make an excuse to go up and put it under the stone.

But at least nothing was said to me to suggest that William had spoken of the incident.

CHAPTER 9

And then the news was brought that Inspector Brunt had been seen about the village again, but we could see no discernible pattern in his movements. Then one day he cornered Stanley and made him late from school. But Stanley invented excuses, so that he did not have to tell my parents that Inspector Brunt had talked to him.

But he told me. We mulled over it like a couple of old folk. The life we led had turned us into premature old folk.

'He reminds me of Dr Fell,' Stanley said. '*The reason why, I cannot tell*—except that the reason why I know full well: you can trust Inspector Brunt to get to where he wants to go. He doesn't seem to mind having to take his time about it. And while he's waiting, he doesn't forget a thing. He's not forgotten a word of what you said to him, that day he met you on your way to Granny Smailes.'

'He talked about that, did he?'

'And about a lot of other things that did not seem to make much sense.'

We were sitting under the wall of a wind-break copse. Even before we started school, we Hollinsheads had learned the art of going to ground.

'Such as what? What sort of things did he ask?'

'Like what was my favourite Sunday dinner. And whether we ever went away for a holiday. And what it's like having a sister who's a teacher.'

'One of these days he's going to ask Lilian questions. Then we shall find out how clever she really is.'

'What had me worried was that I couldn't see what he was trying to get at. He kept asking me the same question more than once. And then he'd pretend that he hadn't heard the first answer properly. And he'd get it all wrong, and I had to keep putting him right, or I'd have been agreeing with something I hadn't said. He was trying to get me to change something. It's all over, once you've told a lie to Inspector Brunt. Once he knows that, he has you where he wants you. He tried to turn me inside out about Dad's pipe-tobacco.'

'What about Dad's pipe-tobacco?'

I felt as if I had ice in my veins.

'Oh, he just wanted to know what sort Dad smoked. And he kept bringing it round to *Prince of Wales*. Did I know anyone who smoked *Prince of Wales*?'

I knew then that before long my turn would come.

In fact it was William who next came in for a round of questioning, and that raised a pretty picture, for even Inspector Brunt would have to work hard to get anything out of William. William was not fond of speech. Certainly he never saw any necessity to explain himself or his thoughts to anyone in the family. He never mouthed a sentence when a single word would serve: and he saved himself a monosyllable when a grunt would do. So what Brunt could get out of him escaped Stanley and me. We were not, of course, told anything about the interview.

But there was a strange incident concerning William that was enacted in front of us all. Two or three days after the Inspector had talked to him, William was away for the inside of a day, driving three beef-bullocks to market. He came home with a watch in his pocket: an object such as none of us could imagine being owned by anyone but my father. With hindsight I can say that it was a cheap, nickel-plated, ugly-faced time-piece, but we caught our breath when William casually brought it out during the course of the evening. It was new. It had an extra-ordinarily loud tick and its black Roman numerals were enormous.

My father looked up as William had it in his hand, pushed himself out of his chair and held out his hand for it. He tested its weight in his palm.

'Did Brunt give you the money for this?'

'No.'

My father slowly shook his head in disbelief, waited for a few moments for William to say something in self-justification, then half turned, half stooped and pitched the watch into the reddest part of the fire. The glass cracked suddenly in the heat. And then, grotesquely, the hands curled upwards and outwards from the dial before they melted.

Two or three days later, just as we had got home from school, Lilian was upstairs changing out of her teaching clothes, the youngest were quarrelling in the corners, and my mother was in the dairy, busy with sour milk and muslin bags. Outside, the bell rang at the shed, and there was a time when Lilian would have been downstairs and across the yard in seconds. But John Palmer belonged to a past about which she was still angry. My mother put her head round the door.

'Kathy!'

As a rule I would have needed no persuasion. My nosiness usually got me to callers first. But there was no eagerness in me today. Since my meeting with Mr Fred, I had barely been able to stand my own company.

'Kathy!'

My mother was also near to breaking-point. I went without hurrying. There was no guarantee that I would even be polite to a stranger.

But when I saw who the stranger was—

Inspector Brunt was actually smiling. His smile sickened me more than any expression I had seen before in those anaemic eyes.

'You aren't afraid of me, surely, Kathy? It isn't so very

long that we took a little walk together and you were very helpful indeed.'

I stood in front of him speechless, unable to look him in the face. The infant in me almost took over and I wanted to run into the illusory safety of the house. But his voice really did sound like that of an ordinary man.

'All I wanted was a pot of tea, Kathy—and a little something to eat. Just something to take the edge off a raw afternoon—a slice of bread and jam, perhaps.'

'You'd better wait in the shed,' I said, and escaped indoors.

My mother was back in the kitchen, already filling the kettle.

'Is it anyone we know?'

'Inspector Brunt.'

She wiped her hands. It struck me what a pale, suffering woman she was.

'You make it. I'll take it out to him.'

She went back into the dairy and tidied up her half-finished cheese-making. By the time she came back I had the tea and the jam sandwich ready. Lilian remained upstairs.

My mother was out of the house for what seemed an age. I could not apply myself to anything. I even went and stood near the back door in the ridiculous hope that I might be able to hear what the voices were saying. It must have been twenty minutes before she came back—and even then, it was no further than to the door.

'It's you he wants, Kathy.'

And—this made it seem even harder to face—it was clear that she intended to come back into the shed with me. It was bad enough to have to tell lies to Inspector Brunt; to have to tell them with my mother standing by was more than I thought I could manage.

I saw that Inspector Brunt had drunk only a mouthful of his tea and had not touched the bread and jam at all.

He looked at me with his false amiability.

'Inspector Brunt wants to ask you some questions,' my mother said, and then, as if to take the sting out of it, she herself asked the only one that mattered.

'How come you've been buying *Prince of Wales* at Mrs Harrison's?'

The inspector did not stop smiling. And as I reconstruct the incident, I must admire his self-control. By getting in first, my mother ought in theory to have left his sails sagging.

I tried to think. It was no use trying to deny it. Mrs Harrison must have told him about my purchase. I was not devious-minded enough in those days to suppose that he had visited all the village shops in our area, asking to be told about unusual sales of that particular brand. But if I admitted buying the stuff—

'So you've taken up pipe-smoking, have you, Kathy?' he asked benignly.

But I could see that my mother was finding nothing to smile at.

'No, sir.'

'Then who was it for?'

I had not yet admitted buying the tobacco—but we had bypassed that. There was no point in trying to go back. Silence was my only refuge. The inspector waited. My mother waited. But it was Inspector Brunt who knew the next move to make.

'It was for Uncle Fred, wasn't it?'

Why did he get that wrong? And why did it anger me when he said *Uncle* instead of *Mr*? Again I stayed silent.

'So tell me when you saw your uncle, Kathy.'

His tone was still silky, but there was a trace of hardness creeping back into it. He was warning me that he was going to stand for no evasion. My mother was looking at me intensely. I tried to read some message in her eyes, but they told me nothing. She was pale, taut: but she gave no clue as to what she was really thinking.

'Sir, he isn't my uncle.'

'Of course. You told me that before. What is it you call him? I've forgotten—'

'Sir—Mr Fred.'

'So when did you see Mr Fred, Kathy?'

This time there was no doubting that he meant business. It was his last offer of friendliness.

'Sir, I haven't seen Mr Fred since—'

'Since when, Kathy?'

'Sir, since people have been saying he's hiding somewhere. Sir, I haven't seen him at all.'

My mother was breathing regularly and audibly with her lips parted.

'So if you haven't seen him, how come you bought him tobacco?'

Up to that second I had been wondering what I could answer to that. Then I was truly inspired—one of those gifts with which the skies occasionally oblige.

'Sir, it was to be a present. Sir, I remembered that he liked *Prince of Wales*. And I meant to give him a packet when I did see him, sir. Sir, I've tried looking for him.'

Inspector Brunt took this in, and there was the briefest of gaps before his next question.

'So what put *Prince of Wales* into your head last Saturday of all days, Kathy?'

'Sir, I don't know.'

'No, I don't imagine that you do, Kathy.'

He was heading me into another of those side-alleys where I might admit something without speaking the words. If I did not stand up to him now, the whole story was going to be peeled apart: Lilian and John Palmer, and the tea-party with Miss Hargreaves that Miss Hargreaves did not know about. I repeated myself.

'Sir, it was for a present. Sir, I was going to give it to him when I did see him. Sir, I've been looking for him.'

'Well, well, well—so you have, have you? Kathy, you and I ought to have a little more trust in each other. We seem to be going through life trying to do the same thing.'

He was the only one who found this amusing. My mother and I saw no humour in it.

'So how much did it cost you, Kathy, an ounce of *Prince of Wales*?'

'Sir, fivepence.'

'And where did you get fivepence?'

I could see how tensely my mother was waiting for my reply to that.

'Sir, out of my money-box.'

'I should like to see your money-box, Kathy.'

I wondered what point he saw in that. My mother was quick to move across the shed.

'I'll go and get it.'

Inspector Brunt was so sly and efficient that I have thought ever since that it was a mistake on his part to let her do that. Perhaps he did not attach much importance to it. Perhaps he thought that he and my mother were of one mind about the money-box. Perhaps he simply underestimated her.

Our money-boxes were kept on the kitchen mantelpiece. They were made of tin, shaped like GPO pillar-boxes—and we all resented them. Very rarely did one of us ever come by a penny, and when we did—if there was one in our stocking at Christmas time—we were almost always made to 'post' it. But there was a way in which a patient and determined child could extract a coin by inserting the blade of a table-knife through the slot. The only trouble was that we had to be careful not to leave a tell-tale bend in the metal. Stanley had once had a sore backside on that account.

From the shed, my mother could get to the kitchen mantelpiece and back in about six seconds; and six seconds was all she took. But somehow or other she must have got her hand on a table-knife on the way. She handed the money-box to Inspector Brunt and his eye rested at once on the misshapen red metal under the slot. He shook it, rattling the few coins that it held. But they told him nothing.

'Bad commercial practice, Kathy, to liquidate your capital.'

'Sir?'

'Never mind. It's your money, after all. But let me give you a little free advice.'

There followed a lecture about the dangers of playing with fire, with strong insinuations about Mr Fred. But no details were supplied, except for something that I did not believe.

'It might interest you to know, Kathy, that at least three little girls were never seen alive again after they had taken tobacco to your Mr Fred. And in two other cases it was cough-lozenges.'

He sent me indoors and my mother spent a few more minutes with him. When she came back into the house, she called me at once into the dairy.

'There must be milk dripping all over the place.'

But there wasn't. None of her tubs and buckets that she had set to catch the drips were anything like full. But she closed the door behind us.

'Kathy—I just don't know what to make of you.'

She gripped me by the upper arms so tightly that it hurt.

'But you're to tell me—because I know—where did you see Mr Fred?'

'Up by the limekiln.'

Futile to have tried to conceal that.

'When?'

She snapped it at me like a gunshot. And this was the crucial question. I had admitted much, but at all costs I must conceal what Lilian and I had been up to last

Saturday afternoon.

'A long time ago,' I said.

'That isn't an answer.'

'I think it was two Sundays ago.'

'You *think*—'

'It was the day William dug out the badger.'

It was the first time in my life that I lent reality to a fib by adding irrelevant detail.

'What have you done with the tobacco?'

'I've hidden it.'

Either she overlooked the point, or she did not care—or she was too good a psychologist: she did not ask me where.

'Go and get it.'

I did. I felt certain she would destroy it—throw it perhaps to the back of the kitchen fire.

But she slipped it into her apron pocket.

Other things began to happen. Inspector Brunt was seen about the neighbourhood with other men, whom the village did not know. Soldiers pitched bell-tents on a flank of hillside adjacent to the Four Acre—and we were forbidden under the direst threats to go anywhere near them. Sometimes we were aware of strange faces looking at us over the perimeter walls; but they always stayed scrupulously on the outside.

My father changed some of the things that had become a habit with him. His lunch-box no longer went for unaccountable outings. He seemed to be working these days always near the house. And he stayed at home on the day of Buxton market. There was no reason that Stanley and I could see for that: no seasonal jobs to keep him at home.

Then came an evening when we knew, although of course not a word was said in explanation to us, that something grave and final had been planned. We had not seen my father since we came home from school, and then, as soon as we had eaten, my mother and William went out, separately and with an interval between them, my mother carrying a bundle wrapped in old sacking. Only a few minutes after she had left, William came back again. He looked at us sheepishly, lifted my father's gun from its bracket on the wall and took it with him out into the night.

Lilian had obviously been ordered to keep us under trebly strict discipline, but even we doubted her interpretation of it. Doubtless it was her own state of nerves that was making things worse for us. She insisted on sending the younger ones to bed three-quarters of an hour before their normal time and then, outrageously, proposed the same for Stanley and me. We tried to reason, but there was no mistaking her mood. She was ready to tear our limbs from their sockets if we resisted her.

Stanley and I quietly met on the landing, and I asked him what was going on.

'Obvious. They're getting Mr Fred away. Haven't you seen all the strangers about? They must have this place besieged.'

Stanley was almost a ventriloquist.

'And it'll not be easy. They'll have to be up to some tricks.'

'Tricks?'

'Like making noises in the wrong place. I'll bet they'll make them think he's escaping down through the Steep Wood. Then when Brunt and his men move down there, Mr Fred can make for Baldlow.'

'But suppose the whole place is surrounded?'

'Didn't I tell you two to go to bed?'

That was Lilian, tearing open the door at the foot of the stairs. She had my father's razor-strop in her hand.

We went back to our own rooms and I stood moodily at

the window, turning my back on Emily and Caroline, who were sniggering about some stupid nothing with the sheets pulled over their faces. It was pathetic how untouched they were by the true gravity of the night.

I tried in vain to make sense of the darkness outside. There was no succession of intelligible sounds: simply a pattern of heaving silence with the usual nocturnal noises off. The wind whined in branches near and distant. A gate creaked on a loose hinge, maddeningly unrhythmic. A she-cat was calling in a corner of the yard. The bucket clanked against the coping of the well. It ought to have been taken off its hook at the end of the afternoon.

There was no way in which I could have got out of the house, otherwise I would have faced the elements. Most of all I wished I could get my hands on that precious tobacco of Mr Fred's and find some way of getting it to him: some way that would let him know that it was my doing. I pictured him, vividly, in his cloth cap, flat on top, but with the peak at a jaunty angle. I had heard my parents say that his leg was stiff because of lead shot in the muscle that had not been taken out after an accident in a shooting-butt. That was why he stood with his walking-stick against one hip, leaning out at an angle at one side, his lame leg counterbalancing it on the other. That was how he would be standing now, on some hillside, peering out into the night. Or would he be on the move by now? When Mr Fred was in a hurry, his stiff leg did not seem to impede him. I thought of him striding over the saddleback of Baldlow.

I had looked everywhere for that packet of tobacco, after my mother had taken it from me. The most likely place had been an old tea-caddy on the highest shelf in the kitchen. That was where she always put things that she wanted to keep from us children. I had had to stand on a stool on a chair to reach it. But the tobacco was not there. I thought then that perhaps she might have put it in with one of his lunch packets. If so, would he guess that it was I who had bought it for him as he had asked?

I strained my eyes at the window, but it was as black a night as I had ever seen. I had heard a horse whinny in the middle distance. And then I heard other horsemen riding up, noisy, at least half a dozen of them. It sounded as if they were coming here for certain. But as I waited for them to halt at the gate, they rode on past. They must have come from the head of the Steep Wood and be heading now for the Dumble.

Then, suddenly, a shot. It sounded as if it came from the Gulley, a minor ravine of outcrop stone that ruined the centre of the hayfield. Just one shot: a shocking stab of sound in that dark solitude. It set cows lowing in their stalls, and I heard Brindle, somewhere out in the void. Men's voices shouted in two or three places. I heard the band of horsemen stop, then they turned round and began to canter back.

Then a figure came into the yard. I could see by the light from the kitchen window that it was my mother—but she looked completely different from the mother I knew. She had no hat. Her movements were darting and purposeful: she seemed to have cast aside her normal staidness. Most astonishing of all was that she had Brindle with her. She had no liking for dogs at all, had as little to do with them as she could, surely an unusual attitude for a farmer's wife. It was the only time in my life that I ever saw her with one on a leash. She bent down and seemed to be having difficulty unhooking the collar. But almost at once my father and William came into the yard together and William helped her. She held the gun while he struggled with the awkward fastening.

Then they came into the house, and hardly a minute too soon, for the place was suddenly alive with men. Lanterns played on faces that were wholly strange to me. Orders were shouted. The kitchen door was thrown open and stayed open, the yellow light falling in a triangle over the cobbles. And then the small crowd parted, and something was being carried into the house across that triangle. It was a shapeless bundle, carried on one of the hurdles from the sheep-pens. I knew that it was a man and I knew—how do we come to know such things for the first time in our lives?—that the man's greatcoat had been pulled up to cover his head and face because he was not decent to look at. I knew that that man was dead—and I knew that the greatcoat was Mr Fred's. And I wanted to break every law and rush downstairs, but suddenly the stairs-door opened and Lilian, pale and speechless, was ushered up by my mother. She would not tell me anything. I think that she genuinely could not speak.

Men came and men went, men's voice droned in the room below, until they became part of the healthless sleep that eventually overtook me. Nobody told us anything that had happened. But somehow in the morning it seeped into our certain knowledge that it truly was Mr Fred who had been shot, and that Inspector Brunt had taken William away.

CHAPTER 10

It was not the custom in our family to burn midnight oil while the future was discussed. On the morning when we were going to break up for the Christmas holidays, I was told that this was to be my last day at school. From now on I was to help in the house. I had a glimmering of hope that this was going to put me into a new relationship with my mother. I think I actually believed that there was going to be something approaching equality between us. With the children all at school, with baby Thomas asleep, with Walter playing round some corner, my father out mending walls and counting sheep, we would have the inside of every day, my mother and I, for talk and companionship. One day she might even talk to me about Mr Fred.

I had no hankering to stay at school. It was part of the understood Hollinshead plan that I shouldn't. One day, it was expected, Lilian would finish her studies (she never did) and then everything would be concentrated on prolonging Stanley's days at school.

I was glad to be sidling out of the classroom: the desk-tops with the grain worn into ridges, over which it was impossible to write properly (but you were caned if you didn't.) But as we stood to sing 'Now the day is over', I stood between desk and bench, crying unashamedly. I quickly parted myself from the others as we spread up the Dumble, clutching paper garlands and heavily crayoned Christmas cards. I did not even want Stanley's company today.

Christmas passed, and the High Peak winter was less harsh than the average. We had a week or two of snow, but never enough to keep the children from school. Then followed a sodden February, the turf squelching up round the welts of our boots. Mud encroached into the kitchen as if it had a will of its own, and chasing it out again seemed to have become the pivot of my life. And any special relationship with my mother seemed to have become a vain dream. We became little more than running enemies. She seemed to consider herself duty-bound to keep me disciplined. She seemed unable to see that there might be more ways than one of doing the ordinary things about the house. Even the way I held a broom became a bone of contention.

Relations with Lilian changed too. For all the mollycoddling and air of distinction that my sister managed to wring out of her book-learning, she was jealous of me. I was nearer to the heart of hearth and

home than she was. I do not know what privileges she
thought I was cornering, but everything I did seemed
suspect to her, and she compensated by treating me as if I
were her servant as well as my parents'. And she had a
further claim to superiority: she was now a member of the
inner council in the affair of Mr Fred. Alongside my
mother and father she was going to travel to Derby in a
few weeks' time to give evidence at William's trial. But
the details were all kept rigorously from me. I put a foot
wrong if I even showed curiosity.

I was kitchen-maid, dairy-maid, laundry-maid,
seamstress and yard-girl. I had to blacklead the range and
keep the copper boiling, skim milk and turn cheeses,
sweep under beds and in closets, boil pigswill, scrub
eggs and change the straw in the nest-boxes. It became
one long round of carping and recrimination. There were
days when I did nothing right, when I began to think that
my mother must be regretting her decision to bring me
into the house. I tried to make allowances for her newest
pregnancy. Her regular child-bearing was as essential a
part of the rhythm of our life as it was of hers.

It did not occur to me to consider how much the
forthcoming trial was preying on the nerves of those who
were going to have to go into the witness-box. It was not
until the eve of the actual day that Lilian, tense and
almost panic-stricken, had to share a confidence with me
in spite of herself. As had happened before, she called me
over to the table on which she had spread her books. She
had not written more than a line and a half all evening.
She propped her forehead against her fingers, half hiding
her eyes. I was convinced that she was over-dramatizing.

'I don't know how I'm going to face tomorrow.'

I did not well over with natural sympathy.

'I suppose you can only answer the questions that
Inspector Brunt asks you.'

'Dolt! It won't be Inspector Brunt. It's out of his hands.

This will be a lawyer: wig and gown—and a judge in red robes.'

'You can only answer what they ask.'

'Knowing what's going to happen to William? Knowing that I'm going to help to make it happen? You know what it is they're going to ask, don't you? You know what it is I'm going to have to tell them?'

I shook my head. How could I know anything?

'Don't you know I've got to say that after they'd all gone out that night, William came back into the house for Father's gun?'

Breakfast was before dawn the next morning. I was told the previous evening that I was to cook it for everyone. But nobody wanted any. I did my honest best to be useful, but only got into everyone's way.

It was a morning of solemn clothes, my mother in a rustling black satin dress that I had only seen her wear at a great-aunt's funeral. Lilian looked like a fully grown woman in a two-piece costume with a double-breasted coat: something old of my mother's that she had altered for her.

It was a long day: March—a rough month that seemed not to know that it would officially be spring in a week or two's time. I had work enough on my hands until I had got Emily and Caroline away to school. For the rest of the day I flogged my brain with doom.

The assize witnesses were very late returning. It was nearly midnight when I heard wheels up the track. The three came into the house with physical fatigue heaped on their barely tolerable trauma. I behaved warily. I could see myself all too easily becoming the target of three people's accumulated bile. When we got to bed, I tried to get news out of Lilian. But she would not be drawn.

'Just tell me what's happened to William.'

'Don't be silly. Nobody knows yet. The jury aren't even out.'

The jury did retire before the end of the week — though I did not know of it at the time. But there came a day when my mother and father went again to Derby. And this time Lilian did not go with them.

The day after that, my father and I were first down in the kitchen, as had become the pattern since I had left school. We greeted each other tolerantly, but we never conversed.

This morning he was shaving with a cut-throat razor at the sink. And this was unusual. Except on market days, he did not pay attention to his appearance until the end of the working part of the day.

'They are all to wear their Sunday best at the breakfast table. There is to be no talking as they come downstairs. There is to be reverent silence round the table. Go and tell them.'

I noticed then that he had put on his best white shirt and his black trousers. I went towards the stairs, but had to wait for my mother to come down. She looked at what he was wearing.

'You mean to go through with this?'

'I have said so, have I not?'

'You know what I think. I shall play no part in it.'

'I would have expected you to. He is your son.'

She did not reply to this, but he neither lost his temper nor pressed her further. It was not easy for me to persuade the others that the message I took them was to be taken seriously. They thought it was some sort of horseplay, of which, a few months previously, I would have been well capable. Lilian and Stanley, however, knew what it was all about. I went downstairs and saw that my mother had made no move in the direction of the range.

'Have I to get them their breakfast?' I asked.

She nodded vaguely, without looking at me.

'What shall I give them?'

'Bread and water,' my father said.

My mother turned her back on him and went out into the scullery. When we were all at the table, he fetched the prayer book and the family Bible from the shelf and began to read aloud.

'*Take therefore in good part the chastisement of the Lord, for whom the Lord loveth he chasteneth and scourgeth every son whom he receiveth. Forasmuch as it hath pleased Almighty God of his great mercy to take unto himself the soul of William Needham—*'

He stopped reading to turn his head and look at the mantel clock. It stood at a minute to eight and he held up his hand for silence. If we had had a clock that gathered itself for action with a deep breath of clicks and whirrs, I would be able to quote A.E. Housman at this point. But our chime was cheap, tinny and extraordinarily rapid. I can't claim that I thought much about it at the time, but the moment was etched cruelly on my memory. It has often struck me since that it was a cheap, tinny and incongruous commentary on an abruptly terminated life.

From the scullery there came not a sound. I think probably my mother had let herself out of the house, but I have never known for certain. She did not appear again until after the children had gone down the hill and my father was out in the fields. When she did come in, she made no remark at all to me, but worked vigorously and noisily for the first half of the morning.

My father, when the stroke of eight was done, went to the shelf for his pen and ink and drew a line through one of the names in the register on the fly-leaf of the Bible. He wrote something down—only a few words: but I had often noticed how laboriously my father wrote, and how the product of much diligent scratching was often not more than a word or two.

Only when he had finished this did he allow us to touch our food. The children had to go to school in their sober finery, the subtlest misery of all, for every family in the village must surely have known why. Stanley came home with his clothes in an appalling state, as if he had rolled in them in the stony road. The Wardles—or the Ollerenshaws. He never told us, and my mother did not ask him. She did not reprimand him. She ushered him upstairs and told him to get himself changed before his father came in.

PART TWO

CHAPTER 11

Sometimes men and women do things that are difficult to account for; and if it is not for money or for fame, then it is likely to be concerned with sex. In order to ensure that our desire to reproduce ourselves does not flag, we have been given certain emotional machinery. We do not always recognize that machinery, even when it is at its busiest. We do not always understand what is going on. We are so jealous of our sexual processes that society has invented hypocritical codes to prevent our taking proper stock of them. The nineteenth century was particularly prone to this. I am writing this in my eighties, and I might be expected to take an old-fashioned attitude to sex. To some extent I do. There is a contemporary tendency to rob sex of its privacy, and perhaps even this is better than false shame—or than pretending that we are not as other people are. But there is something that goes against the grain with me. An act of love is personal to two people. It is a secret that they share. They make their own discoveries, they invent their own play, they have their own fun and they arrive at their own moments of overwhelming satisfaction. It all belongs to them and to them alone, and neither before nor after is their behaviour anyone else's business.

My life changed when I was twenty. The watershed came at a time when I could not visualize that anything was ever going to change. It was then that a man took charge of my life. He educated me — not all of a sudden. He took me away from Kiln Farm — the biggest step of all. He gave me a home which, thanks particularly to his calling, it was especially easy for us to fill with fine things: including many books. He was patient with me when I went astray in my search for things to value. We were exactly ready for each other. We loved each other too consumingly for there to be any ultimate hindrances between us. We made our intimate discoveries together, we invented our own play (perhaps it was not so very original!) — we enjoyed our own fun. And at moments we were overwhelmed. That is all I propose to say about that side of our life.

But I am saying it because I cannot believe that there was ever such a relationship between my mother and my father. And here I go: having insisted on the privacy of my own memories, I have to go on at once to explore someone else's!

My mother bore nine children, which made her no exception in her times. But people who are shocked by the large Victorian families sometimes forget those babies that the mothers did not have. If there were three years between a pair of my brothers and sisters, this does not mean that my mother was not pregnant during the interval. Throughout my childhood I took it for granted that she would occasionally suffer from undefined illnesses. She would have a day—or two—in bed. She made temperamental demands for privacy: at least, we would have called them temperamental if we had happened to know the word. There is no need to remind ourselves that nowadays women do not go on having baby after baby in the way that she did. I didn't: I had two. But my mother was only following the pattern of her day; it would be too easy and totally unjust to have expected her to be more enlightened than anyone she knew. Moreover, there was a phrase used by married men—I hope, though doubt, a good deal less nowadays—who spoke in terms of their *rights*. Of course, it is a phrase that I never heard my father use; but it is surely one that belonged to his outlook. Sometimes I have wondered whether, if I had been married to a man like that, I would have conceded the existence of such *rights*. But it is very easy to be independent out of context. Men were the key to bread, butter, such security as the future held—and to domestic peace.

I married John Palmer. He was twenty-six when I was twenty. I did not court him in competition with Lilian. She had resolved never to forgive him for forsaking Kiln Farm when he did. (I may say that John, as son and heir and already junior partner of a large family firm of auctioneers and estate agents, came and went a good deal about the countryside, and was always well informed about what was going on.) Lilian liked not forgiving people; but she underwent an earthquake of jealousy when she saw which way things were going between John and me. I found that very gratifying.

It was about six months after the beginning of the First World War that John Palmer and I met again. It was in 1909 that my brother William was hanged, and in the years since that I had devolved into one of the fixtures of Kiln Farm. I was always making up fantasies of escape, but for one reason or another I always fought shy of the decisive move. I had a strong sense of duty towards my mother, which somehow survived her irascibility. I thought of what might happen to the younger ones, if I were not there to keep things stable. My sister Emily would have taken over my role if I had defected. And she was a whining, unconfident, lethargic child, who could tolerably ply a broom but could never be relied on for any initiative.

So Kiln Farm continued to subsist. The winters were hard, and 1911 was harder than most: the farm cut off even from the road for six weeks. The vagaries of farming hit my father more harshly than average: cows went sick from eating frosted turnips and sheep suffered from the black quarter. At special times, like our pettifogging haymaking, all capable hands in the family were turned out, but for the most part my father tackled everything himself, there being no money to offer a hired hand. My mother kept the books—or, rather, the book—for there was nothing complex in our profit and loss account, and it was not often that the pounds column of our weekly turnover rose to three pounds. Poverty was often spoken of and on some reckoning days destitution must have been close. We never actually wanted for a meal, but there must have been days when my mother could not forecast tomorrow.

She had never, I could now see, been a happy woman, but in my younger days she had at least made some effort to keep the babies amused. Now even this seemed beyond her. Either she had forgotten how to smile—or she no longer thought there was any point in ever doing so. In general, though, she kept control of herself. There was one occasion when she was out of the house for so very long that even my father showed himself worried. We supposed—I still suppose—that she had gone off in some sort of fugue. I doubt whether she actually left our own hillsides. When she returned, after five or six hours, she was neither more nor less distressed than before she went. Indeed, distressed is perhaps too strong a word to use. She bore her misery placidly and never said anything to communicate it to others.

And even in her misery, she maintained her dignity. There were standards that she could never have yielded. She would never have tolerated uncleanliness. It was a constant skirmish in those parts of the house that had direct access to the yard and every bedroom had to be faultless. We were all made—*taught* would be a happier term—to look after our clothes and produce miracles from remnants.

The outbreak of the war made no tangible difference to our outlook. We were not in touch with neighbours who could feed us ideas or shake our faith in the permanency of everything to which we were accustomed. We still did not take a daily newspaper. Lilian, now working as an uncertificated teacher in a village in the opposite direction from Waterlow, came home with scare-stories. But then, she did that, war or no war. We were unaffected by the wave of patriotism that swept the country. We did not speculate about the length of the conflict or the prospects of ultimate catastrophe. The assault on gallant little Belgium meant no more to us than any other piece of transient London news. It was only Stanley, now apprenticed to a pipe-layer, who came home with overheard phrases that belonged to a world outside ours: *atrocities, just causes* and *right over might*.

In March 1915 we were still feeling no personal pinch. Could anything have persuaded us that we could have been pinched further? The nearest we had so far come to sacrifice was when an elderly remount officer came scouting for horses; he took one look at my father's working animals and passed on to the next farm.

Then one day the bell tinkled outside our refreshment shed. I rapidly changed my apron, tying the bow behind my back as I strode for the door. There were troops training under canvas on a hillside two miles from us and they came sometimes for cups of tea. There had so far been no caller with whom I had readily fallen in love, but I did not need telling of the possibility. Sooner or later, with or without merit, it would have happened.

But standing by the kitchen door now were three officers: saddle-soaped belts, immaculate brown boots and angelically smooth-shaven cheeks. They were blue-prints for gallantry and I was so startled by their dashing smiles that I let them see me flustered as I took their order.

'Now just take slow, deep breaths and the floor won't open to swallow you up.'

Only when he spoke did I recognize John Palmer. His uniform had the effect, paradoxically, of emphasizing both his youth and his authority. Back in the kitchen I spilled water on the fire as I set down the kettle, knocked the loaf to the floor as I reached out to cut it, somehow smeared butter over the back of my hand. It was with a heavily loaded tray that I returned to the shed and there were three pairs of hands so eager to make work light for me that they got in each other's way and mine too.

Did I suspect that Second Lieutenant John Palmer had brought his friends here in the first instance in order to show them the scene of a murder that had made national news not much more than five years ago?

'Now which of the sisters are you?' he asked me.

'I'm Kathy.'

'Never!'

He looked at me frankly, though with his mouth open, half comically, yet not with any sense of mockery.

'What was it you tried to make me do once? Recite the alphabet backwards?'

Still he did not give the impression that he was making fun of me.

'I bet you couldn't do it, anyway, John.'

This was one of his companions, and then all three of them began to try to do it, confusing each other as they all talked at once.

'Do you know, I really believe I would have to have it written down first. You'd better give us a demonstration, Kathy.'

I did not want to at first. It seemed an idiotic thing to stand doing in front of three army officers. But there was something so gleefully genuine about their clamour that I let myself be persuaded.

'It's easy if you try to make a sort of poem of it,' I said. 'Z, Y, X; W, Vee; U, T, S; R, Q, Pee—'

But I went wrong somewhere in the middle. We laughed hilariously, and I said I really must get back to my work in the house.

'And leave me alone with these two wretches?' John said. 'And a disbelief in dreams? Because I am sure that if I am fool enough to let you out of my sight now, you will never come back. I am far from convinced that you are real.'

'She seems real enough to me,' one of the others said. 'Are you real, Kathy?'

He put out his hand to touch mine, and I drew back involuntarily.

'Oh, now, steady! But this was the very thing the colonel was trying to teach us this morning: even a surprise attack needs thorough preparation.'

'I'd say that obviously here is a situation that calls for a flanking movement.'

'Personally, I would rather operate as a lone patrol.'

'With no reserves.'

'There are some encounters in which a man has to be self-sufficient.'

I had by now got to the door and my hand was on the latch.

'That'll do!' John Palmer said to his friends in a tone so sharp that they were taken by surprise. Although they were his equals in rank, there was something about him that made them seem ready to accept commands from him.

'Why don't you come to our regimental dance?' he asked me. 'Saturday night in the village hall at Walldale.'

'I couldn't possibly,' I said.

'What sort of talk is that, *couldn't possibly*?'

'I can't dance, for one thing.'

'Then come and learn.'

'I couldn't possibly.'

'What a consistent young lady you are.'

But he must have detected from my tone that I was not inwardly dismissing the idea. In spite of the impossibilities, I was exploring it. He looked at me with hopeful enquiry.

'I couldn't possibly get to Walldale.'

'Then I'll send transport for you. Would you like me to come in and speak to your mother?'

'Oh no. Please don't do that. Oh, no—you mustn't.'

That would wipe a rag over the whole dream.

'Now look,' he said. 'I am not lightly going to take no for an answer.'

I did go to that dance. When I hear of young ladies who claim they have been done out of things like that by their family ties, I do not believe that they really wanted to go; or else they are made very differently from me. I went by the only means by which I could get out of that house. I simply absented myself without explanation. It was an impulsive thing to do, and the aftermath was likely to be volcanic. The aftermath *was* volcanic—and enduring. But I am an impulsive person—and I knew that this was a moment of decision. I cared less about the aftermath than I did about missing that evening with John Palmer.

He did not actually send transport for me. He came himself—on an army motorcycle. I had to sit on the pillion with my arms about his waist, the only physical means of keeping myself aboard: the war had already loosened a lot of disciplines. It was a blood-stirring ride, villagers standing with turned heads to see who was streaking through with such dashing bursts of throttle.

I wish I had time and space to do justice to the weeks that followed: the haze of bluebells under the pristine green of bursting ashbuds; the car that John borrowed—an open tourer that broke down at the head of the Winnats Pass; the picnic—suddenly seeing John in mufti again after years, by the deep green waters of a privately owned dale to which he had access. It is not a new story: two people, in finding each other, also find things that have been around them all their lives. But that is not what this story is about. This story is about Fred Needham. It is simply that at this period in our lives, there were things that mattered more to John and me than Fred Needham.

John brought up the subject while he was preparing me for my first visit to his home.

'Of course, they do know who you are.'

'I can't think that the Hollinsheads of Kiln Farm can mean much to them.'

Which shows how far gone I was already from my past. John waited for it to dawn on me by delayed action what he was getting at. Then, very quietly, looking at me with his personal brand of sensitive wisdom, he made me understand. He never seemed patronizing, because he had a way of always looking as if he was proud to be with me.

'I'm afraid you won't find many people, Kathy, who don't know all about Kiln Farm—or think they do.'

'But that's long ago, John. And I had nothing to do with it.'

'Granted. I know that. And so does anyone else who thinks about it. But on the other hand, you can't blame quite reasonable people for wondering.'

It was not exactly that I had lived my life so far in blinkers. For the last eight years, I had hardly met anyone but the Hollinsheads. I had not talked at length to any stranger. Since I had met John and been introduced to the outer fringes of officers' mess society, I had been too absorbed to consider what people might be thinking. His kindness, his avoidance of anything invidious in our talk, had themselves been disarming.

'I hope you don't think—'

'Oh, now, Kathy, please know once and for all that it does not matter to me one little bit what happened when you were a girl.'

'I never understood it,' I said, intuitively trying to change the angle. 'I've never understood why William—'

'Well, isn't it true—I hate to say this, but let's clear things out of the way while we're about it: isn't it true that your brother William was, well, not as bright as he might have been?'

This was hurtful. I didn't believe it. No one at home had ever made any such suggestion.

'There was nothing wrong with William. What are you trying to say: that he was mental? He was all right when you got to know him. Oh, I know he had very little to say. But people who do talk a lot aren't always all that much—'

'Now, please, Kathy, don't think I'm saying anything against your family. I'm just letting you know what you must expect people to think. And he certainly gave that impression at his trial. Even though he didn't go into the witness-box, did not speak a word, the figure that he cut in the dock was—oh well, never mind, perhaps it was part of his defence. What else could his lawyers have found, other than try to prove that he wasn't responsible for his own actions? Unfortunately, the jury thought otherwise; they had very little to go on but the way he sat scowling at them. The judge must have taken against him, too, otherwise there'd surely have been something in his notes to the Home Secretary that would have got the poor devil a reprieve.'

This was a mass of things that had never occurred to me.

'It was all a terrible tragedy,' John said. 'The country was aghast. I don't think, right till the last moment, there were many of the public who did not believe there would be mercy from Whitehall. Certainly the national press—even the *Morning Post*—was on his side. To the leader-writers, the issue was simple. They always are happy when they are saying what people want to hear. One of them actually wrote that William Hollinshead had rid the High Peak of a monster.'

'Mr Fred was not a monster,' I said.

'Oh God—don't tell me you're going to leap to the defence of Needham now?'

'Mr Fred—'

'I wish you wouldn't call him by that silly name.'

All the time I had known John Palmer, my greatest inner fear was that I would put him off by being silly. There were often times, I knew, when by his standards the things I said must be silly. I knew that John Palmer had had chances, learned things that had never come my way. I knew that the Palmers were *toffs*: that was the word we used in those days to denote a social stratum to which we had no access. It represented an entity that was very real to us. I knew that John Palmer and his officer friends even spoke an English that was different from mine. Yet never once in all our time together did he ever show sign that he thought himself superior to me.

But—

But I could not give way to him over Mr Fred. I am not

by nature a tearful person, but my eyes filled with tears at this moment: because I saw the collapse of the entire dream.

John was at once concerned to repair the damage.

'Please, Kathy, let's forget it. It hasn't anything to do with us. It never was anything to do with you. You just happened to be there, to grow up with it all round you.'

'I never was able to believe the things that they said about Mr—about Mr Needham.'

'Well: you could be right. He was never brought to trial—though he didn't improve his image by escaping from remand. Who are we to set ourselves up as judges without evidence? But the reason I've brought all this up is this: tomorrow afternoon, you are coming home with me.'

'I don't want to, John.'

'Please, Kathy, listen to what I am going to say.'

'I know what you are going to say. I know I shall do all sorts of things wrong. And they are going to sit looking at me and thinking about William.'

'Nothing of the kind—well, let's be brutally honest: something of the kind. But Kathy, it really isn't fair of you not to let me finish what I'm trying to say.'

So I made a little stupid drama of closing my lips tightly and looking at him with as noncommittal an expression as I could muster. I looked so silly that we both burst out laughing. And after that he went on more easily.

'You mustn't blame my mother and father for wondering, Kathy. Anyone would wonder. My mother, particularly, is bound to be just a bit frightened. I mean, I know there's nothing in it, but what mother would not be just a little uneasy to see her son marry—'

He halted, unable to find words that were not too raw. I looked at him sharply. It was the first time between us that marriage, as a word, had been mooted. And he had said it with such matter-of-fact certainty.

'The sister of a murderer,' I said, tonelessly.

'Let's not exaggerate the connection. A murderer's half-sister. And if there's to be argument about it, not the half that matters.'

I looked at him sharply again, this time because I did not understand at all.

'What do you mean?'

'What do I mean?'

And then a new truth dawned on him.

'Oh God, you don't know, do you? You don't know anything. And yet you've got to know.'

'I have no idea what you are talking about.'

'No, you haven't. And that makes you more innocent than ever. Well, for better or for worse—we shall be saying those words in public soon—William Hollinshead was Fred Needham's son.'

'I don't believe it.'

Nor did I. Nor could I.

'There isn't a great deal of point in not believing it, Kathy. We've still got the newspaper cuttings somewhere at home—of the trial, I mean—and if you want to plough through them, you can. Your mother, under oath, did not try to dispute the revelation. Not that it matters. Not that it's in any way relevant to *us*. That's what I'm trying to say. I'm trying to clear all this nonsense out of the way.'

It did not make sense for me to wish that I had never met John Palmer, but all this was suddenly too much for me. I wanted to run away from everyone. John took both my hands in his.

'Listen. We are going to be married. I haven't asked you your opinion about that, because I know what it is. We both know what it is. Don't we? And I'm certainly not going to give you the chance to say something self-sacrificial that will deprive me, for all the wrong reasons, of—'

'John—'

'My parents are reasonable people. They are good people. They are kind people. But they are confused people, too. They are also very much wrapped up in me. They are bound to be anxious. And in addition to all this, they have already had one nasty shock: they have very mixed feelings about the way I rushed into the army. They are half proud, half apprehensive. And now, on top of that, this—These are abnormal years we are living through, Kathy. The earthquake is all but too much for them.'

'I don't want to come, John.'

'There is nothing for you to be afraid of. Whatever is in their minds, they would do nothing, say nothing, that might make you ill at ease. That is what I am wanting to tell you. All you have to do is be your normal self. They will be charmed.'

'And I'll be scared out of my wits.'

'Don't forget that they'll be at least a little scared too.'

'In case I've brought my shotgun with me?'

'Oh, Kathy—'

I almost defected from that first visit to the Palmers. I hated every prospect of it, not least because I was afraid of committing some gaffe in the drawing-room or at table. But of all my worries, this was the least grounded. In this respect I was underestimating my mother. In her early years she had formed a very firm notion of what was ladylike. She herself had been drilled in an uncompromising school. She may not have heaped fawning affection on us. She may have reeled, mentally and emotionally, for the rest of her life after the shame of her first-born. But she taught us good manners and made us maintain them. She would have nothing else round her.

I knew as John was seeing me home to Waterlow

afterwards that I had not done too badly with his parents. Maybe I did not volunteer answers to those questions that they hadn't the moral courage to ask. But I came as a pleasant surprise to them — and I knew at each stage when I was winning.

For a while life flowed easily and slowly: a deceptive pace. Then all things happened at once. John was posted from his training battalion and given two weeks' leave, which meant embarkation and France. We applied for a special licence, and our wedding was as quiet as the Palmers would allow it to be. Obviously, my parents-in-law were not overjoyed by the speed of events. They must have had strong reservations about their son's wartime marriage, as they had about his immediate future in the trenches. There were few public illusions now about the expectations of an infantry subaltern; but in a way I think this helped them to accept this other aberration of his. And however much I may have worried them, they did not dislike me. True to their idea of living, neither of them ever said a single invidious word to me. And now I saw too some of the material advantages of marrying into a family of estate agents. They had no difficulty in finding me a little cottage to rent in Tideswell Dale: John set such store by my making a home of our own that he could come to on leave.

There were lonely, hideous hours. It is outside the purpose of this tale to relive them now. Sometimes I would stand outside that cottage and look at the stars and face out in the direction in which, four hundred miles away, I knew John to be. And I would pray that he was still alive, and that he would live through another night.

But it is the nature of a pendulum to swing, and my happy memories of Tideswell Dale are more abiding than the intolerable hours.

CHAPTER 12

My father died in 1917—in a manner that had all the makings of a High Peak legend. He was chain-harrowing clods in a field that he would never have dreamed of trying to break down into a tilth but for the exigencies of the war years. He had a stroke and fell across the rusty thumping mesh, whereupon his horse stumbled into a rut and got hopelessly entangled in the tack. Somehow my mother got him home and to bed, where he raved for a week. But it was not Brunt, Needham and his family who were obsessing him now. It was his impossible task in that stone-ridden field, and he was harrowing clods until his last breath, alternately cursing his horse, his harrow and the bedrock.

My mother had a stroke too—of genius. She fixed up reins to the foot of his bed and put the loop of leather in his hands. Night and day until the end he harrowed as if fiends were after him. Within an hour of his dying, his horse died in its stable. In my native neck of the Pennines, people prefer stories to end like that. It would be curmudgeonly to question every sliver of truth.

The war had moved us Hollinsheads around. Caroline, at seventeen, was a trainee nurse at the Manchester Royal Infirmary, and came home for the funeral looking like the soldier's dream of Blighty. Emily, still snivelling, still beset by woes that she scarcely understood, had married, of all people, one of the least noticeable of the Ollerenshaw boys, whom she had brought to live at Kiln Farm.

Lilian was unable to come to the funeral. She had married a bookseller in a residential suburb of Derby. Did I say bookseller? If you dug deep enough through the cards of corn-plasters, the dummy bars of chocolate and the phials of scented cachous, you might have found a *Daily Compendium of Golden Thoughts* or an *Illustrated History of the War* in weekly instalments. Edwin Statham, her husband, had put his varicose veins at the service of the Army Pay Corps and Lilian could not afford to leave the counter behind which she served for fourteen hours a day.

But the showpiece—in the house, in the churchyard and at large in the village—was Stanley, who had got himself into the Royal Navy by using his imagination about his age, and came home from a shore training establishment at Devonport looking as if he might dance a hornpipe at any moment.

My mother seemed to have been buffeted by my father's death into a state of walking coma. It was impossible to know for certain what she was feeling. Grief? Did she grieve for the man who had given her eight of her nine children, and to my uncertain count eight miscarriages? And who had ruled her household with an eye to its joylessness? Was she worried out of her wits by her immediate material prospects. (John Palmer's father was prepared to use his full influence to enable her to keep the tenancy, if Emily and her husband would run the farm.) I had of course offered her a bed in my cottage, but I cannot pretend to have been other than relieved when she unpersuadably turned it down.

Had she been knocked out of proper consciousness by those memories that such an occasion was bound to bring? Could it really be true that she had allowed Fred Needham to make love to her? I say 'allowed', because it surpassed my imagination that she could ever have had joy of it. Surely she and Mr Fred could never have *played*? I could never picture her as candid with a man as John and I naturally were with each other. Come to that, how had she ever accepted my father? What *fun* could they ever have had?

In the early evening she went upstairs to her room, leaving only us youngsters in the farm kitchen. Since my marriage I had not been too dutiful in the matter of home visits, and the sight of all the old objects hit me with a sense of flesh-creeping nausea: my father's carriage whip in a corner, the shoddy old cupboard through which sound used to carry up to Stanley's ears. No one had even thought of removing our old money-boxes.

Our conversation had to return to childhood; even to some of those things which by unspoken common agreement, we normally steered clear of. Somebody remembered Lilian's bedtime stories. Someone else mentioned the first night that Inspector Brunt called. I do not know who was the first to say William's name.

'That dreadful day when Father threw his watch on the fire!'

'Because he thought it was a bribe from Inspector Brunt.'

Then came a cynical chuckle from the corner where Stanley sat. He was actually in his father's chair now, his bell-bottom trousers incongruous above a pair of Father's house slippers that he had found. It had looked appallingly disrespectful when we first saw him put them on.

'Father knew well enough that that watch had not come from Brunt. He knew that Fred Needham had given him the money for it.'

'Why should that have upset him? He'd deserved something from Mr Fred, hadn't he, all the miles of walking he did for him, all the risks that he took?'

I was dying to know whether any of the others had picked up the story about Mr Fred being William's father. But I did not want to take the initiative. If they did not know—or if it was not true—I didn't not want to be the one to pass it on.

'I don't know,' Stanley was saying. 'When you come to weigh it up, there were a lot of things that we didn't know. It used to drive William mad, the things he had to do for Needham when he was holed up here. He said the risks they were taking were beyond all reason.'

'William said all that?'

'In his own words.'

'You must have had a talent for getting him to talk.'

'Oh, he'd talk sometimes—in bed. He never seemed to mind talking so much once the candle was out.'

So then I asked the key question. I could not keep it back.

'Stanley—*why* did William do it?'

'I don't know. I've never known. It's never made sense. Of course, he knew—'

'What did he know, Stanley?'

I knew what Stanley had been going to say. And when he held back, I knew that it was for the same reason that I was holding back. Why fill Emily's and Caroline's and Walter's and Thomas's head with more rottenness than was in them already?

'Nothing. My mind was wandering. I think he just ended up by hating the man. You know how once William got an idea in his head, it took a little shifting. I remember the time he was worried out of his mind by you.'

'Worried by me?'

'Yes, you, gentle Kathy. Didn't he come across you up in the hills one day, sitting on Needham's knee? Wasn't that the day you and Lilian were supposed to be having tea with Miss Hargreaves?'

'He told you about that?'

'The same day. I tell you: he was worried.'

'I never sat on Mr Fred's knee.'

'I wouldn't swear to remember everything.'

'And William never told Mother and Father?'

'No. He said we had enough rows in this house.'

'Oh, do tell us, Kath,' Emily said. She would have had the story buzzing round Waterlow within twenty-four hours.

'Kathy's a respectable married woman,' Stanley said. 'She was only a kid in those days. We were all only kids.'

He got up, went to the door, slithered out of the slippers and stooped to tie his naval boots.

'God, this place gets me down. I don't know how any of us stayed sane. I'm for the tavern. Are you staying much longer, Kathy?'

'Pa-in-law's sending his car up.'

'Don't forget to tip the footman.'

After that, Emily started trying to dig lurid aspects of hospital life out of Caroline. At seven the mantel clock performed its tinny and ridiculously rapid little chime. Before the last stroke, I heard the tyres come to rest in the yard.

As we emerged from the cart-track into the road along which we used to walk to school, I could feel the oppression of those hills lift from me.

CHAPTER 13

The war played itself out at last. We stayed for a few months in the cottage and then moved into the beautiful and solid house on the outskirts of Bakewell in which I have lived ever since. John opened and managed a new branch of the family business and expansive years opened up before us. We had a car of our own now, indispensable for John's work, and John began to teach me to drive. That was how we came one afternoon to the village of Stadlow while their Maytime Wells Dressings were in progress.

Many Derbyshire villages have retained—or re-
vived—this ritual of decorating their wells and fountains
with lifesize biblical scenes depicted by hundreds of
thousands of flower petals laid out against mud and moss.
I had been looking forward to Stadlow for days. But first
John had to go and survey the big house, which was
coming on the market.

'You know, don't you, that as far as you are concerned,
this was where it all started?'

I had no idea what he meant, but it sometimes amused
him to talk in riddles, pretending to perplex me in a
gentle way.

'Stadlow Hall. That's where your mother was lady's
maid.'

I knew that that was what she had been, but I could not
have furnished the vaguest detail. It is astounding how
secretive both my parents were about everything
connected with their history. They had something to
hide—and played safe by trying to hide everything. And I
don't mean simply hiding it from us; I believe they were
trying to hide it from themselves too.

'This is where she met your father,' John said. 'And
your Mr Fred.'

He had once objected somewhat bitterly to my calling
him that. Now as he used the phrase himself, there was a
mischief in his eyes. It signified acquiescence—and was
also an acknowledgement that I had progressed.

'Oddly enough, it was at a Wells Dressing that it all
started. When I was here the other day I met a couple of
people who'd served at the Hall in the old days. They
remembered the three of them well. Well: there was a
fourth. They made quite a name for themselves.'

The Hall in my mother's day had belonged to a retired
admiral. It had passed to his son, who had gone down at
Jutland. Its upkeep was beyond the daughter-in-law, who
preferred her London home. The day of the great

country mansion was beginning to be over. That was how John came to be taking stock of it. And that was why there were some rooms whose floorboards were so rotten that John would not let me walk on them. There were rooms on an upper floor—servants' bedrooms, John said—where the mildewed wallpaper was torn away down to Regency patterns. The view over the garden was of a vast wilderness, made even more pathetic by glimpses of what had once been. Roses had reverted to briar. The shape of the original beds and borders was still discernible in places: golden rod had taken possession of a quarter of an acre of what had once been lawn. The stonework of the great amphora on one of the terraces had been chipped and crumbled by years of frost, denuding the metal bands that held the things together.

'Your grandfather used to be head gardener here.'

'I did not realize that.'

'Didn't your mother ever tell you anything about her younger days?'

'Never anything. We understood it was something that children did not ask about. I could not tell you the first thing about my grandparents.'

'I'm not surprised. Feelings ran high. When people have had to chisel their own dignity out of the bedrock, they defend it fiercely. They'd worked so hard for what they thought they had achieved; it could be wrested from them in an instant. Perhaps you'd rather I didn't talk about it?'

'On the contrary. It's time I knew.'

'You're not going to think I've been spying on your family affairs?'

'Oh no, John.'

He did not immediately embark upon a narrative. He seemed to be thinking about it still. But when we went into one room, upstairs, at the front of the house, he remarked that my mother must have spent many hours in here. It was the private drawing-room—the holiest of feminine holies.

'Would a maid spend much of her time in the private drawing-room?'

'A lady's maid would. Lady Marsden was notoriously withdrawn. I don't think she got much of her life's joy out of the admiral. Her maid was an important part of her life.'

'She could be, I suppose.'

'She was. I heard that explicitly.'

'I see. That explains a lot. My mother's standards—'

'Yes. I hate to use the phrase—but standards improbably acquired. Forgive me if I seem to be putting it crudely. It's a credit to your mother that she did cling jealously to what she'd learned.'

I looked round that room. It was impossible to recreate it as it must have looked in those hours that she had spent in here. There was only one article of furniture left: a chair too rotten to appreciate. But the view from the magnificent window was unchanged. There was a line of wooded hills beyond a broad, fertile valley. Near at hand I saw the striped canvas and bunting of the travelling fairground that was part of the village jollification. Had my mother sometimes looked out of that window and wanted to escape? To escape from the elderly female fug into the air of those hills? To go down to the laughing crowd round the tinselly stalls and mechanical organs?

'What sort of woman was Lady Marsden?'

'There's plenty of first-hand testimony about that. Very independent—I mean of mind, not just material wealth: though that too. Very scathing of anything that fell short of what she saw as sense. Very strict on moral issues. Demanding of loyalty: but appreciative of it too. She was the sort of woman who would have treated your mother as an equal—just as long as she never claimed equality.'

I saw what he meant. By 1920 we thought ourselves

splendidly liberated. But my mother was also a strong
character. I could not see that she would care to be
treated feudally. I said so to John.

'But remember the contrast with what she'd come
from. Her father had not always been head gardener. He
had worked his way up. During her childhood he'd been
struggling — and with no certainty of success.'

In some labourer's cottage, kept decent against dirt,
damp and pokiness by faith and determination? An
uphill fight: all the way to Kiln Farm.

I will not tell my mother's story as if John unfolded it
for me as we walked round Stadlow Hall. He had not put
it all together yet. For years afterwards we both kept
finding new things to add to it. Some of our sources — one
particularly — were unexpected. Sometimes we had to
coax our imaginations to bridge gaps. But in the final
count, I would like to think that John and I did not go
badly wrong with her.

CHAPTER 14

The position of lady's maid could bring unique
advantages. It was also uniquely dangerous. Upstairs, she
had to be capable of anticipating — which meant that in
some respects she had to be quicker-witted than her
mistress. But it could be fatal to let this be seen.
Downstairs she was superior. It was not lost on the
servants' hall that she had the mistress's ear. Other
servants distrusted her — but treated her with self-
defensive respect. By playing her cards shrewdly she could
protect her interests in both worlds. There might be times
when it would pay her off to bear a tale to the drawing-
room; but only if the mistress was a true diplomat.
Likewise, she had to watch that any news that she carried

down the backstairs did not find its way back to the chintzed throne. Favour could be lost by a whisper. And the road out led infamously nowhere.

Lady Marsden groomed Hetty Price at a very early age for the upstairs drawing-room. It was not many years ago that her father had graduated to sole charge of the great gardens. Milady was making one of her bountiful rounds of the cottages when she noticed a child with her hair in a white bow. I have a posed photograph of my mother at that period. Lady Marsden at once saw the potential, gave the girl some discarded books to read, met her and talked to her again by contrived accident. One afternoon she invited her to come upstairs—to play with her, one might almost say, for she gave the child the run of her pots and showed her how to mix a face-lotion.

Hetty was lady's-maiding before she was ready for the full run of her duties. But Lady Marsden was taking a long-term view. She was content to do some things for herself in preparation for the time when she would have to be dependent on an attractive and mature young woman. But by the time she was eighteen, my mother was working at full function. She had been so well drilled—at home, as well as at the Hall—in the tactics of her position, that she made no mistakes on either side of the servants' door: not that that saved her from sometimes being suspect.

In fact she was generally regarded as too toffee-nosed ever to make a real friend at the servants' table. But this can hardly be put down as Hetty Price's fault. Lady Marsden used a lot of skill to make her into what she wanted.

Her ladyship often sermonized when the two were alone together. Like so many who set such public store by their ivory integrity, she took pleasure in surveying the depravity of others. She had a remarkable intelligence system about the estate and the village, never missing a downfall or a pending downfall. She was acidulous in her condemnations and had no difficulty in training her maid to think as she did.

Up to a point: but Hetty had her limitations—not glaring ones—hardly worth labelling shortcomings. But there were weak spots. The education that her mistress had given her could not go deep enough to offset all the inclinations of a marriageable girl. My mother did not exactly lack taste—she was learning all the time—but sometimes she gave herself away. She might show her liking for a grossly sentimental picture; or be caught humming a street-level ballad. Or she might giggle over something that a lady ought not to consider funny.

And she sometimes looked wistfully out of the window, at the hills or the village couples arm in arm.

Now Lady Marsden's principal amusement came from the manipulation of other people's selves and young Henrietta sometimes came in for subtle torture. Nothing gave Lady Marsden greater pleasure than to read Henrietta's mind—especially when her thoughts were at variance with the spirit of the drawing-room.

Lady Marsden caught sight of the remote look in the girl's eyes as she looked out over the lawns to where the flags and awnings of a travelling fairground were visible through the trees. It was late May. The wells had been dressed overnight and blessed by the vicar that morning. There was a relaxation of discipline in the servants' hall—an annual concession that had come to be held as a tradition. Almost the entire staff would be down in the village, where there were maypole dancing, try-your-strength machines, brandy-snap and a booth where cannibals danced. Naturally, Lady Marsden held herself aloof from such occasions—and needed the company of her Henrietta.

She saw the look in the girl's eyes and made idle sport of it.

'Oh for a magic carpet that would waft you down among the vulgar throng!'

It was the third year in succession that Hetty had not even caught a glimpse of the decorated wells.

'You're just aching to get down there, aren't you?'

'No, ma'am.'

A surge of crowd laughter rose from behind the greenery. In spite of herself, Hetty made a slight movement of her body at the window, trying to see something of what was going on. It was not lost on her mistress.

'Well, don't let me stand in your way. Go along if you must, dear child. I shall probably fall asleep presently.'

Did she mean it, or didn't she? If Hetty took a step towards the door, it would be quite in character for the old lady to burst out in condemnation of her common taste. She turned her back to the window, looking uncertainly at her mistress.

'Well, go on, be off with you! I've given you leave of absence.'

'I think I will go down there, just for half an hour. You're very kind, ma'am.'

It seemed a long walk across the room. She expected to be called back at every step, to be made to stand motionless for a tirade against her vulgarity. But for once Lady Marsden seemed to have meant neither more nor less than she had said. Hetty went and put on the lightest coloured coat she had, and her newest hat—both, in all conscience, on the puritanical side for capering on the green. She felt unsure of herself as she walked along the drive. A music hall song was being jangled out of a street organ. She saw two of the Hall servants—Evans, a groom and Doris Something-or-other, a wretched-brained little kitchen-maid, disappearing hand in hand over the railings of a plantation. But even that dim-witted creature had somehow got herself finery for the occasion— something stridently pink and fluttering.

Hetty reached the village and walked carefully, trying to avoid being bumped into. A capuchin monkey in a little vivid green suit pushed his crabbed little face into hers, carrying a tin collecting-cup. A man on stilts strode perilously close to her, yellow flowing trousers over legs seven feet long. A nostalgic hot smell of boiling sugar came from a confectioner's stall, where a man with mutton-chop whiskers was pulling and kneading a viscous toffee mixture on a hook.

A beery man, his breath sour across her face, tried to get his arm across her shoulders. She side-stepped and pushed him away. He lurched backwards as if he were going to fall, then righted himself and pushed his face into hers.

''S all same to me. 'S all same to me.'

She tried to get away from him but was jolted from behind, thrust up against him. He made a fuddled attempt to touch the brim of his hat.

'It's all same to me, lady, if it's all same to you.'

'Go away!' she said.

'When a lady comes to a fair—'

Again he stretched out his hand towards her and this time she had to move crab-fashion to get away from him. Then two determined and sturdy young men came up alongside him and each gripped one of his arms above the elbow. One of them was a dour and craggy-looking man in a dark coarse suit, his eye steadily on her as he handled the drunk. The other was wearing a flat cloth cap and carrying a walking-stick. He raised its handle to face level as he touched his cap to her. She looked into his face: a broadly smiling, angelically smooth face, with full red cheeks and eyes that were calling hers their equals.

'You'll give us half a minute, miss, to dispose of this varmint. Then we'll be back.'

They were away less than three minutes.

'Thank you,' she said. 'But I hope you didn't hurt him.'

'He'll come to his senses a sober and cleaner man,' said the one she was presently to know as Fred.

'What have you done with him?'

'We've dressed the horse-trough with him,' said the man on his left, called Will.

And each taking an arm, they began to propel her towards the afternoon's gaiety.

Their expertise seemed to be universal. She stood by them while they hurled wooden balls into the voluminous jumble-sale clothes of an Aunt Sally. She watched them shatter a row of clay pipes—but only after they had picked up and examined every rifle in the gallery. They won things for her. They heaped trophies into the crooks of her arms until she had more than she could carry: a plaster squirrel, a panoramic view of Matlock Bath encrusted with sea-shells. At the hoop-la stall, the man had apparently already had costly experience of their skills, for he warned them off and would not let them play. At another booth, they paid for her silhouette to be cut from a shadow thrown on a screen.

'A lemonade, Hett?'

There was a sharp acidity about the drink that seemed to symbolize the world that she had been missing all her life.

'I shall have to be getting back,' she said.

'Back? You've only just come.'

'Some of us have work to do—our daily bread to earn. I must be back at the Hall by tea-time.'

'Oh, you're at the Hall?'

'Yes. I'm—'

Then some inner voice told her that they would not think better of her for being lady's maid.

'Well, if you must, you must, I suppose. We'll walk you to the gates.'

It was Fred who did most of the talking, obviously the

leader of the two, but Will was no stick-in-the-mud. What these two got up to in their wanderings about the countryside must have the makings of an epic.

'You're in the kitchen, I hope,' Fred said. 'That's the one thing we've never had so far—a friend in the kitchen at Stadlow Hall.'

'No, not in the kitchen,' she said, letting them see that she was going to be enigmatic about it. They did not seem to care enough to press her. When they reached the drive gates they released her arms, but obviously wanted to stay talking for a time yet.

'So—we shall have to make arrangements to get together again.'

'Aye,' Will confirmed.

'I hardly ever get time off.'

'Everybody's entitled to time off.'

'Yes, well—then I have to go home.'

'And where's home?'

'Stadlow. My parents live on the estate.'

'They do, do they? Your father isn't a gamekeeper, I hope.'

She had to laugh at the mock horror that passed over Fred's face. But she still felt chary about identifying herself.

'You haven't even told us your other name. I'm Fred Needham. This is Will Hollinshead.'

She saw something extraordinary in the man. She could not have said what it was. There was a vitality and a decency about him that one did not encounter in every face. There was an originality about him. He was not as other men were. And there was a challenge in the way that he was looking at her. If she did not tell him who she was, she would go down in his estimation.

'My name's Price.'

'The gardener's lass?'

'That's right.'

Fred looked at her as if he suddenly knew a good deal more about her than he had a few moments ago. Something inside her wilted at the thought. Fred Needham and Will Hollinshead would know people in the servants' hall. They would not have heard much in favour of Hetty Price. But Fred Needham seemed to sense what she was thinking. He put a reassuring hand on her shoulder.

'If you're Bert Price's girl, there'll be nowt much wrong with you.'

Will Hollinshead also smiled thinly into her eyes and nodded vigorously.

'Anyhow, if there's anything in the offing, we know how we can get in touch with you.'

It seemed unlikely that she would see them again. She wished them goodbye and walked towards the house, wondering whether they would still be standing looking after her. She did not turn her head to see. It was only when Lady Marsden sardonically asked her what scenes the floral artists had put up this year that she realized that she had not actually seen any of the wells.

John said that he had done as much as he could in Stadlow Hall for today, but he would have to come back, and I could certainly come with him if I wanted to.

We drove along the white dust of the drive. So my grandfather had once had the planning and command of these grounds? The weeds had pushed the stone slabs of the paved walks out of alignment. Convolvulus had overgrown an ornamental pagoda, and some of its tiles were missing. As we passed through the gate-posts—the gates themselves had gone—I tried to picture my mother standing there with those two men. It was purely an academic exercise. I knew that her true self must elude me. And what complicated matters further was that the only Fred Needham I could conjure up was the one that I knew.

My mother had never met any other man like him. She was haunted by his eyes and smile. I could not rid myself of the idea, probably unjustified, that like me she was haunted by the angles: the racy way he wore his cap, the picture of readiness for anything that he presented when he leaned on his stick.

'You're in love!'

Lady Marsden said it after the third clumsy mistake that Hetty had made in one day.

'Who is he?'

Hetty busied herself with a tray at a sideboard and did not turn round.

'All right, don't tell me if you don't wish to. I shall find out, of course. I presume it is someone you met at the fair. No wonder you had no time for Old Testament tableaux.'

When my mother could no longer avoid looking round, she saw that the old lady was laughing. She had sounded wholly embittered.

'I suppose now you will start asking me for time off.'

Lady Marsden performed a parody of a sigh.

'We shall have to consider that. Of course, there will be no favours until you have told me the name of your beau.'

Hetty did not tell her. And she abandoned any hope of seeing the couple again. She did not even know whether they were Stadlow men or not. She guessed that their time was pretty busily occupied—and that largely in happy roguery. They had probably forgotten her by now. But she was overlooking the impact that she herself might have made. She was doing a few trivial needle-work tasks one afternoon while Lady Marsden was resting when one of the housemaids came up to the drawing-room.

'There's someone asking for you in the kitchen yard. A man.'

The girl giggled adenoidally.

'Did he say who he was?'

The girl sniggered again.

Hetty knew that every pair of eyes must be on her as she passed through the kitchen. She went out into the yard and looked about for Fred Needham. Then a dark-clad figure came out from where he had been standing half hidden by a rain-barrel: Will Hollinshead.

'Oh, hullo,' she said, not caring whether her tone was offhand or not.

'Good afternoon, miss.'

Why was he not calling her by her Christian name now? She did not prompt him to. His eyes would not stay on her face. He was behaving quite differently from the other afternoon. She did not understand his personal brand of embarrassment.

'What can I do for you, Mr Hollinshead?'

Now she was talking as stiffly as he was.

'Fred and I—well, on Sunday we've got the loan of a carriage. We thought perhaps you—'

'Sunday? Sunday isn't my day off.'

'Oh.'

'I only have one Sunday a month off. If I'm lucky. And I told you—I go home to my parents.'

He looked at her dully.

'Maybe we could manage another Sunday.'

'I'll have to see. How can I get a message to you?'

'You can always tell Tom Scragg.'

She was tactful enough to suppress a shudder. Tom Scragg was a coachman at the Hall. In no one's eyes was he a gracious light of the establishment. He had notoriously little control of his thirst or tongue. If private plans were to be committed to Tom Scragg, they could surely not stay private long. It is a wonder that my mother did not take a second and decisive look at her new associations, when she knew that they involved Tom Scragg.

But my mother seemed to have metamorphosed into a different personality. She was in a fever that reduced her ordinary prudence to shreds. She agreed on the intermediary: there was no other way that she could see of finding herself in Fred Needham's company again. Like daughter, like mother: seven years before I came into being, it was remarkably similar to the impulse that took me off to a dance at Walldale on the back of an army motor-cycle. She considered no consequences beyond her immediate intention. Another Sunday was suggested and she made up some paltry and hopelessly unconvincing excuse for not visiting her parents. That was a lie that had to find her out—and it was the beginning of a breach that was never healed. Only the great Sunday mattered. Beyond that things would presumably look after themselves.

She wrote a note and handed it to Scragg for onward transmission. It was not until the Sunday morning early that she had a reply through him: and she had to demean herself by going into the stables to ask him for it. Every servant in the Hall, down to the meanest laundrymaid, knew that the lady's maid had gone into the stables.

She was to be at a crossroads half a mile out of Stadlow at half past ten. She was there; and had to wait twenty minutes for Fred Needham and Will Hollinshead to drive up in an open landau. It was a splendid carriage, in prime of gleam and polish. And the men looked as if they owned it. There was in fact an aura of candid illegality about the whole outing and she let herself enter whole-heartedly into that spirit. I suspect that most 'criminals' have felt a swell of illusory liberation at that moment when they find themselves first irretrievably outside the law. In fact, Fred and Will had 'borrowed' their landau

with the connivance of a caretaker-groom in the absence
of its owner, who was away taking European spa waters.

There was only one cloud on Hetty's horizon on that
ebullient Sabbath, and that was the discovery, stridently
obvious from the moment that the carriage drew in sight,
that she was to have three, not two companions. Gloria
Mason,   buxom,   painted,   shrill,   uproariously   and
outrageously happy, sat on the driving seat with Fred. She
was wearing a fluttering summer dress in an aggressive,
unnatural, poisonous metallic green, against which the
springtime foliage of the dales appeared to shrink and
wilt. And she had on a hat to match—a monstrous,
gargantuan,   cacophonous   creation   whose   ribbons
streaked behind her as they tore past meadows hazy with
May flowers.

At her side Fred Needham was spruce in a tightly
buttoned Norfolk jacket with knee-breeches: new clothes,
that he could not have worn more than a time or two
before. Hetty took the inside seat, beside Will
Hollinshead, whose consort she was evidently to be for the
day. He was wearing darker and older clothes than Fred
and seemed to have lost even such shreds of vivacity as he
had been able to display at the Wells Dressing. He had
been tongue-tied enough the other day, when he had
come to meet her in the kitchen yard. This morning he
was so embarrassed by her presence that he could barely
bring his eyes to rest on her. Love strikes different people
in different ways.

Hetty's first reaction was crushing despondency. But
even in the depths of her first disappointment her fighting
mechanisms were at work. The elemental female in her
saved her from putting a foot wrong. (If, in 1915, I had
had to fight Lilian for John Palmer, might I not have
been capable of complex guile?) And even with Gloria
Mason's envenomed greenery at his side, Fred Needham
was not beyond twisting his head over his shoulder to

smile his broadest smile at Hetty Price. And that gave her more than hope. It crystallized her determination not to accept the *status quo*. Who, after all, was Gloria Mason? She had been on the scene before my mother had heard of any of them, but this gave her no prescriptive right to permanency. The situation needed strategy—and a very liberal helping of opportunism. If she were to succeed, she clearly saw, the last thing she must do today was to alienate anyone. She must especially beware of letting the reputation of the supercilious lady's maid taint these new relationships. Her new friends would be on the lookout for that. They would have heard of her. They would have made their own enquiries (perhaps of the likes of Tom Scragg.) But in the outcome, they would treat her as they found her. She must take good care about what they did find.

If it had merely been an escape that my mother was making, I could make an ironical comparison. When I broke away from Kiln Farm, I was wrenching away the ball and chain of something intolerable. My mother's position at Stadlow Hall was monotonous and irksome—but nothing worse. It was the blinding light of Fred Needham that was dazzling her. And her instincts guided accurate scheming.

She was sweetness itself to Gloria Mason—who, she discovered obliquely during the course of the morning, was a barmaid at Stadlow's Stonebreaker's Rest. She had had to be on duty at her beer-pumps on Wells Dressing afternoon, which was how the men came to be roaming the fairground on their own. And she was a natural iconoclast: a tearer-down of pretentious idols. She did however tend to make the mistake of considering pretentious everything outside herself. She could tear down other people's standards undeterred by her own emptiness: she had no standards of her own to put in the place of what she destroyed. She was a laughing, shrieking mocker of the world about her: a mocker of stuffed-shirt gentry and obsequious labourers alike. She laughed alike at the clothes of dowdy people—and of those who thought they were aping high fashion. Hetty envied the self-satisfied independence of these friends. It was an adorable breakaway from the repetitious 'standards' of Lady Marsden. For the time being it was worth putting up with Gloria Mason's ostentatiously possessive way of clinging to Fred Needham's arm, even when he was reining them round hairpin bends.

Hetty also remembered from time to time to try to pump some conversation out of Will Hollinshead. It seemed odd that Fred Needham should choose such a man as boon companion. Perhaps Will became a different character when the pair were out midnight poaching. Perhaps Fred Needham preferred a friend who was malleable in his hands. It was obviously Fred who was the catalyst. In Fred's company, things started happening to people that did not happen to them when they were on their own.

They lunched at an inn. They lay in the sun on the bank of a broad green valley where the musk grew wild. Fred and Gloria disappeared into a hollow from which she reappeared an hour later with her hair untidied and bits of grass clinging to the sleeves of her dress. During this time, my mother sat at a discreet but not unfriendly distance from Will Hollinshead on the turf and tried to coax him to talk about himself. The nearest he came to fluency was a working description of a new patent safety-trap for stoats and weasels. In the first fading of evening light, he surprised her by producing from an inside pocket a mouth-organ on which he played 'The Maid of the Mill', a sweet, sickly ballad that seemed to draw a haunting peace from the lengthening shadows. (What would Lady Marsden have said about that?) Perhaps Will Hollinshead was hoping that his music would speak those

things that his tongue could not find courage for. My
mother knew the state of his mind, but she was toughly
insensitive to the real sincerity of his feelings. There was a
limit to the outside light that could penetrate her own
inner turbulence. Did she find Will so unattractive that
she was quite unflattered by his worship?

When, in the landau going home, he finally summoned
up the boldness to lay his hand over her knuckles, she let
it lie there. But things went no further between
them—despite the example of Gloria and Fred, who were
now so uncompromisingly close to each other on the
bench up front that a nervous passenger might have
feared for the safety of the carriage.

They dropped Hetty off at the crossroads at which they
had picked her up. They would gladly have taken her to
the Hall gates—and even through them—but she insisted
that her homecoming must be as secret as she could make
it. She gave Will's hand an instantaneous little squeeze as
she left him. Perhaps that was a mite of conscience
money. She stood still and listened to the wheels receding
in the darkness. It took minutes for the last trace of sound
to vanish.

She had half a mile to walk home. And God knew what
seismic upheavals lay in front of her—the total
destruction perhaps of all the foundations on which her
world rested. She knew that she had lost the day, could
not believe that there would come another day to fight.
Fred and Gloria belonged to each other; and Will must
suffer in silence until he either gave up hope or found
someone else who roused him.

Obviously I have had to rely on imagination in some
aspects of this narrative. Perhaps my own character is
illuminated by some of the features that I have supplied
myself. But in the final count, I do not think that I have
badly erred. John has read through what I have written,

and does not think that I have been extravagant. We agree about the general state of affairs that had been reached when my mother got home from her second outing with Fred and Will.

But we were now puzzled—and we remained puzzled for a considerable time. Fred Needham was a man with a mind of his own. He was kindly. He was whimsically independent. He was sentimental at appropriate times. He was probably no great genius at reading other people's more refined reactions. Will Hollinshead was an enigma. There was probably much about him that my mother did not discover until after they were married. He was a man who let his passions smoulder slowly, like charcoal under sand. The more he brooded, the less attractive he was likely to appear.

And now that her first bid had failed, my mother had to account for herself to her parents. It would surely not be long before she would have to be accounting to Lady Marsden too.

These were the circumstances in which she was going to get herself pregnant by Fred Needham. Yet Fred was nevertheless to go on to marry Gloria. And my mother was destined to marry Will Hollinshead and come to Kiln Farm. It was easy to find an explanation in broad theory, yet impossible to come by details. These were things about which even the servants' hall had had to be satisfied with speculation. John and I ended up by giving up realistic hope that we would ever be the wiser.

But information sometimes comes from sources that one has overlooked.

CHAPTER 15

Three or four times a year John had to go to formal dinners staged by organizations with which he had to do professionally. One such was held in Bakewell in 1922 and I was invited. The occasion was a retirement of someone highly placed in the service of the County Council. Service was bad at our end of one of the sprigs. Food was cold before it reached us. The speeches were predictable and hypocritical. I knew none of our immediate neighbours at the table and felt no joy when John left me after the meal to go to talk to some business contact. Two or three minutes later, he came back for me.

'Someone over there I think you'd like to meet.'

He took me to the far end of the top table, now mostly deserted, and I saw there a round-shouldered little man in a charcoal-grey suit who was looking mournfully down at the litter on the tablecloth; abandoned menu-cards, crumpled paper napkins and cigar-ash spilled over from the ashtrays. John stood back to let me approach him alone. He looked up when it was clear that I was coming to speak to him, but there was no spark of recognition from him. Indeed, though his was a face that I would have thought it impossible to forget, I was not even certain about him at first. The sight of him was a shock. I had no way of knowing how old ex-Inspector Brunt now was. It was more than twelve years since I had last seen him, and in the manner of a child I had formed a very exaggerated notion of his age then. Wens, pimples and carbuncles he certainly still had, but even they seemed to have paled into the weary flatness of his face, as if they were part of the professional paraphernalia for which he had no further use. I found myself staring rudely at his eyes, to see if their rims were still red. But perhaps since his retirement he had spent less of his time in the raw open air. Looking back, I think that the greatest difference in him was that, although he was not well dressed, nor wearing well what clothes he had, he looked cared-for in an unambitious way.

'Inspector Brunt?'

He raised his eyebrows and looked at me, but did not stir from his huddled posture in his chair. Obviously I meant nothing to him, and this should have come as no surprise. John encouraged me to look like a young woman of our decade, and my lemon-coloured evening dress with its sleeveless bodice was hardly calculated to recall Kiln Farm. At first I rather enjoyed his puzzled look.

'Don't tell me I've slipped out of your rogues' gallery, Mr Brunt?'

He was not amused by this. He did not look as if he were capable of ever being amused. His air was one of fatigue with the world at all points of contact. It was in fact not a look of puzzlement. It was an appeal to be left alone. I resolved to keep this short.

'I'm Kathy.'

'Kathy?'

'Kathy Hollinshead, when last we met. Kathy Palmer, now.'

He started then to get to his feet, which cost him so much effort that I urged him to stay in his chair. But he insisted on the courtesy and held out a bony but still firm hand.

'Yes. I heard you'd married.'

'I've been Mrs Palmer a long time, Mr Brunt.'

'A long time? Yes—I suppose it seems so to you.'

I got him to sit down again. He looked as if he assumed that all had been said that needed to be said. I felt that I was unkind to go on trying with him. It was an odd experience. He had been my nightmare enemy. Now I felt as if he were an old friend.

'I was scared stiff of you in those days, Mr Brunt.'

He received this thought without enthusiasm; indeed, without acknowledgement that he had heard it.

'I wish we could have a little talk about old times, Mr Brunt.'

He had not only had me scared. His reputation was equally potent among those who had never had anything to do with him: the Wardles and the Ollerenshaws. Up and down the High Peak Hundred you had only to say *Brunt* and men started examining their past mistakes. It was unbelievable that this could be the man.

'I don't think that would be wise, Mrs Palmer.'

'It's just that I never knew what really happened.'

'You think I did, then?'

His tone was too lethargic to be called bitter. But there was something ill-naturedly dismissive abut it that struck a raw patch in me.

'You closed your case,' I said. 'My brother—'

'What happened to him was his fault, not mine.'

'Well, of course it was. You don't think I'm blaming you for what he did, do you? You only had your duty to do.'

I had hoped that this was a gracious admission, but he did not seem to take it that way. Instead, he turned on me the eyes that had once made mine water to look at them.

'I'm sure you would do better to leave it all alone, Mrs Palmer. It wouldn't have come into your head at all, if you hadn't seen me here tonight, would it?'

When I had first recognized him, a minute or two previously, I felt as if we were two people who shared something. But ex-Inspector Brunt was evidently not a man who looked at things in that way. He was a cruelly detached man. I supposed that that was the only way in which he had been able to face up to the largely horrible things with which his life had been filled. He deserved to be left in peace in his retreat.

'I'm sorry to have troubled you, Mr Brunt.'

I am afraid that as John drove me home, I talked too much about Brunt. I could not properly describe what disturbance the man had set up in me.

'I think he was right,' John said, 'when he said it was unwise to interfere with old scars.'

'No. That's not what he was thinking. He meant something quite different.'

John chuckled ironically. 'If you think you know what's in old Tom Brunt's mind, you must have the insight of the century.'

'I ought to have been embarrassed by the sight of him. Instead, it was he who was upset by the sight of me.'

'I think that you're being over-subtle, Kathy. And over-receptive. Old Brunt isn't himself any more. It's like trying to judge a man by his reflection at the bottom of a well.'

'I know. Pathetic. I wish we hadn't run into him.'

'I do hope that we're not going to have Brunt for the remainder of the night.'

John rarely complained in terms as heartfelt as that. I warned myself that I must keep off the subject, and I succeeded in doing so. But it would not leave my brain alone. It thrust itself back into my consciousness within a minute of my unrefreshed awakening the next morning. It was almost a relief to see John leave. The temptation to broach Brunt again over toast and marmalade was almost too strong.

The morning was a humdrum one. I do not want to write anything that will stigmatize me as a bad—or unwilling—mother, but our first-born, Katherine, was at this time at the least fascinating stage. At eight months she was still so immobile that I doubted whether she would ever have the ability—or will—to propel herself at all. An occasional uncoordinated wave-motion of all four limbs seemed to be about her only physical ambition. She was capable of a burble that her father interpreted as *Da* but seemed disinclined for any verbal relationship with me. She had a smile that charmed strangers, but that had me reaching for the gripe-water.

Moreover, today was the day that my bi-weekly help came. I hated her days: I always seemed to have so much work to do before she came, to get the place fit for her to see. True to Parkinson, my work—in an easy house, in which I had more help than I needed—filled my day. I have often thought that the trouble with housework is not that it is hard labour; it is that we do not really believe in it.

It was no joy to me, then, that the doorbell rang while I was still in process of getting everything in the kitchen out of sight before Mrs Burton arrived. I shouted through the house for her to let herself in, but she seemed not to hear me. I went to the door, and it was not locked. But it was not Mrs Burton who was waiting there.

It was Inspector Brunt. He was wearing a respectable bowler hat and carrying a fawn raincoat folded over his arm. Again I had the same impression as last night: that age and retirement had somehow softened down his remarkable ugliness. Although the ingredients re-mained—a globular and shiny cyst over his right cheek-bone—I had to force myself to remember his face as it had looked when he had peered into mine on the way to Granny Smailes.

'May I come in, Mrs Palmer? You must forgive me if I come at an awkward time—'

I was on the brink of starting the welter of work that would fill my hour before Mrs Burton came.

'I stayed the night in Bakewell after the dinner, and need not return to Derby until the eleven-eight.'

I had hardly been aware that he was still speaking. I do not know where my mind had vanished to.

'Come in, Mr Brunt.'

I took his coat from his arm, ushered him into the sitting-room, offered him coffee or tea, but he had just breakfasted.

'I seem to remember you served me a slice of bread and jam once,' he said.

'Which you didn't eat.'

I thought for the moment that we were going to get away to a pleasantly chatty start, but he allowed his face to cloud over.

'I have come to apologize.'

'I can't think what you have to apologize for.'

'About last night. I fear I had allowed myself to sink into a deep-dyed mood. I cannot think what came over me.'

I thought I knew: for a man of Inspector Brunt's activity and self-imposed pressures, the descent into twilit leisure must have left great gaps of frustration.

'I fear I was very rude to you, Mrs. Palmer.'

'Not at all.'

'It was very wrong of me to revive painful memories.'

'But you didn't revive them, Mr Brunt. If anyone started raking through the past, it was I.'

I went and fetched a cloth to wipe Katherine's face. I had suddenly seen with a shock how much breakfast she still had about her mouth. Mr Brunt seemed unconcerned about it. And I feel I must clarify one point. Whatever picture I may be painting of myself, I was not a feckless, not even a bored housewife. It was just that round about this time, I did not seem to be coming properly to grips with myself.

'I know you must blame me for what happened to your brother.'

'I don't blame you at all.'

And that was true. I had never tried to apportion blame in that sense.

'What happened to my brother must, in the final count, have been his own fault.'

'I would not be too sure of that.'

He was a man who had come here with a purpose, though he had not yet brought himself round to declaring it. The business of wanting to apologize was partly true. But I did not think he would have come for that alone. He sat decidedly ill at ease. It astonished me that such a man could be in such an embarrassed condition. Again he started begging my pardon.

'Mrs Palmer, you must send me away if I offend you by bringing up things that are done with.'

'But are they done with, Mr Brunt? I am not offended. Far from it. There are things I have never understood. Sometimes I cannot sleep at night because I cannot bear not to know.'

This was an exaggeration, but once I had said it, I saw that it had more than a slender basis in fact. Some men might have smiled if I had played into their hands in this obliging way. But Inspector Brunt could only look solemn about it.

'In that case, we might agree to trade information,' he said.

So that was what lay under the surface. In many ways—William's fate apart—we had defeated Thomas Brunt. *I* had defeated him. Even on the night of Granny Smailes, I had won the round: from that day to this he had never *known*. Over the ounce of *Prince of Wales*, the affair of my money-box, he must have suspected that he had been done out of the truth. And Thomas Brunt was a man never to forgive himself for such failures. He was a man who could not tolerate not knowing what he thought he had the power to root out.

Katherine started to whimper. I found her rattle, which she promptly threw to the floor.

'I'll agree to that,' I said. 'By all means let's fill in the gaps in what we both know. Who has the right to ask the first question? Do we spin a coin?'

I ought to have known better than to try to be facetious about it. It was plain that he did not like it.

'To you the honour,' he said.

So I had no time to compose oblique words for it. 'Mr Brunt—you don't doubt, I take it, that William was Fred Needham's son?'

'Your mother admitted it in open court.'

'I know that. All the same—'

'I'm afraid, Mrs Palmer—'

'I do wish you'd call me Kathy.'

'I'm afraid, Mrs Kathy Palmer, that no amount of brain-whipping is going to enable you to alter that fact of life.'

'Oh, please don't think that I am worried over the morality of it—even over the sentimental morality. It's *knowing* that troubles me—knowing how it could possibly have come about.'

He made a disclaiming gesture with his hands, held his head a little to one side.

'There are some things to which we cannot expect to know the answer: things that are and ought to remain private.'

'I know that. That isn't quite what I mean.'

And I suddenly found myself flooding him with what I did mean. I told him all the two's and two's that John and I had put together: the fairground and the excursion in the landau.

'But after that, we seem to run out of information.'

'You'd expect to, wouldn't you—at that stage?'

'I mean, apart from anything else, how did my mother manage all the necessary escapes from Lady Marsden?'

'Ah! Now there I think I can help you.'

'All our sources seemed to dry up at that point. There

was a lot of rumour, obviously, a lot of ill-natured gossiping.'

'Don't I know it? The mighty had fallen. Years ago, like you, I tried to go into it all: perhaps with better resources than you, more experience. What is more important, this was within the lifetime of people in Stadlow—servants and others—who knew things first-hand. It was always my way, you know, to want to find everything out—even a good deal of what was only of secondary relevance. I liked to see the whole scene, the whole person—'

'And?'

He permitted himself the first smile I had seen on his face that morning.

'It is amazing how often these things are a matter of chance. About a month after the Sunday of the landau, Gloria Mason had the misfortune to contract the chicken-pox.'

Leaving my mother and Fred Needham another problem—an easily soluble one—how to detach themselves from Will Hollinshead's company.

'Your Uncle Fred was not one to allow the grass to grow under his feet.'

For once, I was not tempted to correct him. I really did think it rather sweet that there was one thing that he never did seem able to get right.

'But I have to say that neither, for that matter, was your mother. I hope I am not shattering too many dream-pictures, Mrs Palmer?'

'They were shattered ages ago. But the way they set about the business still defeats me. I know how little time off she ever got in that Hall. How she ever managed to get away—'

'She didn't need to. You are puzzling yourself about things that have easy solutions, Mrs Palmer. It does not seem to have surpassed your mother's wits to introduce your Uncle Fred into the Hall.'

He did not look at me as he said this. Perhaps he was still overwhelmed by the thought of me as a child of twelve.

'Good gracious!' I said. 'So why, when she became pregnant, did they not take the obvious course?'

If that had happened, if she had not married my father, I would not have even existed. There was something clammy about the thought. Katherine started to cry. Katherine could not have existed, either. I broke off the conversation to attend to her.

'I have never been certain that your Uncle Fred knew about your mother's condition at the time. Chicken-pox is not, after all, a killer disease. It does not last for ever—or even long. Within a week or two, Miss Gloria Mason was back in the Stonebreaker's Rest—and in Fred Needham's arms, too. She was something of a tigress. And even in the life of a tigress, there are moments of crisis that are especially vital. The creature recognizes them. I don't know how spectacularly weak Fred Needham was. I can guess the strength of Gloria Mason's claws. Your mother must have been outmatched by her. I've no doubt she fought too; but she was too nice, Mrs Palmer, too refined, too thoughtful. She was too dignified to come out on top among the sort of animals she had been keeping company with. Gloria Mason lost no time in getting the banns put up.'

'Leaving my mother—'

'It is impossible to exaggerate the hopelessness of her position. Disowned by her parents, who remained totally unforgiving. I'm afraid that happens all too often—and among no one so inflexibly as among those who pride themselves on their own Christian rectitude. She was hounded by Lady Marsden. I do not think that anything so pleasurable had ever entered Lady Marsden's life before: the self-righteous joy of persecution.'

Mr Brunt went through his diffident actions again,

fiddling with the fabric of his trousers above the knee. Do they call it a displacement activity?

'And I'm not at all sure that I ought to tell you this. I am pretty certain — only facts were hard to establish, because there could have been a prosecution — that your mother went to one of the old crones of the village and got some medicament that might have helped her. Only it didn't. I have often wondered whether the embryo might have been damaged in the process; whether perhaps that is why your brother was not all he might have been.'

I heard Mrs Burton letting herself in at the back door. Should I tell her to forget today? I fought shy of that, set her to work upstairs (my bed still unmade!) I knew that she would be working with doors open, straining her ears for anything that might drift upstairs.

'So along came Will Hollinshead, with his self-sacrifical offer of marriage. Except that in your father's case, it was no sacrifice. I have never doubted that he was irretrievably in love with your mother. But he was a strange man, your father. Your mother can hardly have known the first thing about him, when he got the tenancy of Kiln Farm and took her to live in those bleak, empty hills. There was something about those hills that must have suited his bleak empty soul. It has never failed to amaze me how often like calls to unlike. How was it that Will Hollinshead, fundamentally a bleak puritan, found so much to admire in his opposite, Fred Needham? But then, your mother was in a similar position, wasn't she? There is nothing so unnatural to the human race as puritanism — but how tightly it binds when it does take hold! I suppose a man thinks he's doing something positive, to avoid his damnation for eternity. Yet put Will Hollinshead down in Fred Needham's company, and he became a young hellion.'

'It's hard to imagine.'

'Equally hard to imagine that the same thing must have

happened to Hetty Price. But they both reverted when
they were established at Kiln Farm. I would expect your
mother to have been rather difficult to please: very
difficult for Will Hollinshead to please. I would expect
her, wouldn't you, to lay down her standards at the
outset. Things like going upstairs in his boots, for
example—'

He looked at me knowingly.

'It ought not to surprise me that men and women are
often as purblind as they are. Your father's loyalty to your
Uncle Fred knew no bounds, once Fred Needham was in
trouble. Nor did your mother's loyalty, for that matter.
The pathetic thing, to my eyes and ears, was that they
refused to believe—'

Did I still refuse to believe?

'They refused to believe in the teeth of all the evidence
I showed them. But I don't have to trouble you with those
objectionable things.'

'But they're all part of the final picture, aren't they, Mr
Brunt?'

'I have gone on long enough. You must keep your part
of the bargain. It is my turn to ask a question.'

A neat escape-route!

'All right. But we shall come back to this.'

'As you wish. But what I would love to know, Kathy
Palmer, is what you saw, that night up in your bedroom?'

His eyes, faint, and giving that false illusion of
weakness, were turned on me with a new penetration. I
tried to get under the skin of myself as a child again, even
tried to feel the cold of the oilcloth under my feet as I
peeped through the keyhole. Obediently the image
came—but I cannot say that it was physically real.
Katherine broke out in a new, inconsolable squall, and I
excused myself to carry her upstairs and ask Mrs Burton
to have her with her as she worked.

I paused on my landing: a modern, a 1920's landing.

The necessitous war years had forced fashions back into a hygienic plainness. But it was an expensive plainness, suburban gentility aping cottage simplicity of an idealized kind: reproduction ladder-backs and fumed oak coffers. It was far removed from the landing on which I had smelled Mr Fred's pipe. Here, on the respectable outer ring of a creditable market-town, was where I belonged. The other was far behind me. I was safe from it. But it had been real, nevertheless.

And going back down the stairs to ex-Inspector Brunt, catching sight of him through the open sitting-room door, I wondered how I was going to answer his question. Should I admit to him, with a sickly, pardon-begging smile, that I had known all along that Mr Fred had got into my parents' bed, and that my father was hiding, with his boots on, in the clothes closet?

And, of course, the new thought came to me: how safe was it, even at this range in time, to tell the truth to Inspector Brunt? Could he still, would he still, make difficulties for my mother, for all of us Hollinsheads — if some new angle of truth shed final enlightenment? Was that what the Wardles had meant, when they said that Brunt didn't care if he had to wait twenty years?

I sat down, across the hearth from him. He was in my chair, so I was in John's. So familiar things had an uneasy, unfamiliar look.

'Yes,' I said. 'Well, I saw my father in his nightshirt.'

'Surely, Mrs Kathy, you're not worried about what I'm going to do about it now?'

He was into my pettifogging thoughts with destructive precision.

'In any case, it wasn't that night I was thinking about. I meant the night we came to arrest Needham.'

But they had not questioned me about that night. I had been sent upstairs early. I was out of the way. It was assumed that I could know nothing. I had been positively disappointed at being ignored.

'Why didn't you question us younger ones about that at the time, Mr Brunt?'

'Because we had evidence enough. Because—'

He moved his body on his chair.

'Because the case was, as the saying goes, open and shut. There was no need for infants to be plagued in the witness-box. Your mother, your father, your big sister—the things we had seen with our own eyes—'

And suddenly he changed his tone.

'Besides, I expect you are under the impression that I was the champion of the field—that I was the last arbiter. You probably think that a detective-inspector was quite a force in the land.'

There was something behind this that, naturally, he had never revealed to me before. I wondered whether he had ever revealed it at all—outside, perhaps, his closest familiars—if he had any. Was he bitter about relationships in the police force in his day? Or was he merely bitter about self-imposed imperfections of his own?

'I made my reports. Other people decided what action to take on them. But please don't think I am making excuses—'

'Are you trying to tell me that you have some doubt as to whether my brother was guilty?'

'I took the only possible course by arresting him. No officer could have done otherwise.'

'And you went on to give evidence against him in the witness-box.'

'I did not,' he said very forcefully, and looking at me with such aggression that I wondered whether his mind might be just slightly unbalanced on the subject. 'I did not. Never in my professional career did I give evidence in the witness-box for or against. I gave evidence—of fact. My opinions were not admissible.'

He paused, as if he wanted to be sure that he had left me without doubt.

'I made the arrest. The decision to prosecute was not mine. I arrested your brother because he was the one who had the gun. By your sister's testimony, he had come back into the house for it after your mother and father had left. After the shooting, as we were coming up to the house, we saw him give it to your mother to hold while he tied up the dog.'

'That's right,' I said. 'I saw that through the window.'

'And he had the dog. That clinched matters.'

So why did Brunt seem so anxious to justify himself? And why should it clinch matters because William had the dog?

In any case, William had not had the dog—

'Directly after the shot, we all converged on the house. Sergeant Bacon, who had a patrol of uniformed men on horseback: he came back from the valley that you called the Dumble. Your father, your mother, your brother—they seemed to have come from different spots, from which they had been watching. We knew from which angle the shot had come. We did not know which of the three had been in which location. Their evidence on that point was full of contradictions and obscurity. But we did know that whoever had fired the shot was the one who had had the dog with him, because we had heard the animal rooting through the undergrowth from where the shot came.'

I was silent. Once, years ago, I had been afraid of involuntarily blurting something vital out to Brunt. Now there was no danger of that. I held my tongue—but it was not fear of what Brunt might do: I still could not make up my mind whether he would do anything or not. I was silent because I wanted time in which to think things over. And evidently it did not occur to Brunt that I might have something to tell him on this. He went on talking.

'The decision to prosecute was made *upstairs*, as we popularly called it. I am not suggesting that there was anything insincere about that decision. My superiors believed that your brother was guilty. He himself was inarticulate. Some thought that this might be because he had a bad conscience. It is always easy to think things that suit your book. I have always taken the view that your brother was unlucky with the jury. Counsel for the crown made great play of one point especially: they must not be influenced because he had killed a man with a hideous record. That man's hideous record had never been proven. The judge said the same in his summing-up. Twelve good men and true were convinced of the facts—and, I am certain, believed confidently that the Home Secretary would be merciful.'

He looked at me with pity.

'I told you last night that you would gain nothing by trying to dig this ground over again.'

'It's my turn to ask a question, Mr Brunt.'

He inclined his head courteously.

'Tell me plainly—don't embroider the point—just give me your yea or nay—do you believe that Mr Fred was guilty of the things that were said of him?'

'You want my yea or nay? I never doubted it for a moment.'

'It seems so out of character.'

'As you saw his character at twelve years old.'

'I think I would have known,' I said. 'The day he gave me fivepence for his tobacco. I think a child's innate sense of evil would have told me something.'

'He met several children who evidently did not have an innate sense of evil. I think you are talking about fanciful things there, ma'am.'

I had read, in the album in which the Palmers had pasted them, the newspaper cuttings about Mr Fred's so-called crimes, printed at the time when he was on the run. They had meant very little to me. It was a world that I knew only by repute. There were some sexual offences that Queen Victoria used not to believe in, and I think there was a touch of that in my make-up. Moreover, the language was equivocal. The essential *alleged* was repetitive. Nothing seemed convincing. Mr Fred was alleged to have interfered with little girls. He was alleged to have persuaded little girls to interfere unnaturally with him. He was alleged to have raped little girls, to have done them disgusting damage, to have killed them afterwards. To cover up his tracks? In a frenzy of panic? Or a frenzy of God knows what else?

In more than one case, an errand to fetch *Prince of Wales* — or a pennyworth of cough-lozenges — had been part of the routine.

My Mr Fred? With his red smooth cheeks and his almost invisible eyebrows?

Clearly, Mr Brunt hated talking about this kind of thing. Clearly he did not think that even as a married woman of some seven years' standing I could begin to know what it was about.

'I don't understand how a man comes to commit that kind of crime,' I said.

'But we cannot deny that it all too frequently happens.'

'Aren't you condemning him with no chance to defend himself?'

'I know what his defence would have been. We did have him on remand, you know, before he escaped. And we knew that things had gone badly between him and Gloria Mason; as anyone could have predicted. She was not the woman to be satisfied by one man. Sometimes she must have driven him frantic; now with jealousy, now with frustration. And so much of the key evidence against him came from her, you see. Not that that could have been used in a court of law — but it gave us some useful indications while we were investigating. She told us about absences from home at times. She believed that he had been in the Belper area when one child was killed; definitely not far from Beeley, ostensibly poaching, on another crucial night. Needham was going to say that this was all part of a monstrous conspiracy: a scheme to get rid of him, cooked up by Mrs Needham and her fancy beau of the moment.'

'And are these—these perversions supposed to have started after his wife had begun to enrage him?'

'We cannot say that. There will always be crimes of this nature. There always will be. We cannot blame Needham for every indecent assault that took place in Derbyshire during his lifetime. We would have charged him with one. We would never have known for sure about dozens of others. But don't try to find excuses for him, Kathy. A man doesn't have to excuse himself for having been born with hammer-toes, or any other deformity. Why can't we think the same about a man with a mental deformity?'

'I'm sorry,' I said. 'I can't make myself think of Fred Needham as mentally deformed.'

'It's a pity you have to think about him at all. Think instead of the damage he did. And there were other little girls, you know, who weren't killed. You can be sure there were some who didn't even complain. They took his sweets or whatever, and they did what he wanted them to, and they didn't frustrate him, and he didn't go blind with rage.'

I expected the penetrating look again then, but his eyes came nowhere near my face.

'I'm sorry, Kathy. I know all your life you have wanted to believe in him. I have to tell you to that the wave of attacks against girls simply stopped after he died.'

'But you said just now, there might have been lots of men making attacks.'

'I mean, of course, attacks on what we came to call the Needham pattern. Again, I'm sorry, Kathy.'

I had had another question ready for him. But I did not ask it.

'But it was my mother who had the dog with her,' I told John that evening. 'She, who could never stand dogs. And Brindle wouldn't allow her to put her back on the chain, because dogs couldn't stand her, either.'

'You could have been mistaken, Kathy. Perhaps the dog had somehow rejoined her on her way back to the farm.

'Brindle wouldn't. If Brindle had been loose, she'd have gone straight to William, if he was about. If not, she'd have come back to the yard.'

'So why on earth should your mother have the dog?'

'I can't think. Perhaps my father wanted her to have protection.'

More than once, John had been irritated when Mr Fred had obstruded into our lives. Tonight he only wanted to help.

'In any case,' he said, 'it was definitely William who had the gun.'

'Don't ever stop reminding me of that, John. And there's one other thing that I don't understand—I never have understood. Why, John, did Inspector Brunt and his superiors never bring an action against my parents on a charge of harbouring?'

'There could be various reasons. It could be because your parents, your brother—Mr Fred himself—were all too clever for them. Brunt and his colleagues may have known what was going on—but it could be a long haul from there to having a case that would hold good in court.'

'But surely, the way the three of them were wandering about that night—'

'On their own property? Understandably inquisitive when their fields are milling with police? Nothing proved.

The police don't like losing cases in court. They don't like publicizing their own ineptitude. Besides, I think they were only too happy to let the state of affairs go on. It was, after all, leading them to Mr Fred. It *did* lead them to Mr Fred.'

How devious might Brunt and company have been?

'There's another possibility. I don't know whether it's ever occurred to you. What would you have done about things if you'd been in your father's shoes?'

'What would I have done? What else could he have done?'

'With your mother's relations with Mr Fred being what they used to be? And your mother taking a new interest in him?'

'No, John—I won't have that.'

'I won't stress it, but I could make out a case. Think it over some time: walks round the fields in the late afternoon; a red handkerchief under a chair—'

'My father would never have betrayed Mr Fred. Nothing could be less likely.'

'So unlikely that it would have been easy to get away with.'

'I'll never believe that, John. My father *loved* Mr Fred.'

I could easily have become angry about that. John knew so much, and yet essentially so little about the Kiln Farm days. I did not feel that I had ever made them real to him. He smiled at me in a way that had resolved other situations in our time.

'There is another possibility. I've often wondered if Tom Brunt didn't have a soft spot for you Hollinsheads.'

CHAPTER 16

It was six years later that I read in a corner of our local weekly that Thomas Brunt had died. Lost in a whole page of obituaries, he had been considered worthy of an inch and a half. And most of that was taken up by a list of mourners and senders of flowers. There were no reminiscences, no summary of his career. And yet had not the man been a phenomenon in his day? Had he not deflected crime for a working lifetime over some three hundred square miles of limestone hills — as much by his legendary name as by his assiduity?

I found it strangely touching to learn that he had had five children. How much had they seen of him, and he of them, during his day and night vigils, with the dews of the Peak seeping through to his skin? What was Mrs Brunt like, and how keenly had she shared his consuming concern for his job? Had he talked to her about it in the evenings, as John brought home to me the gossip of the auction-room? What could she have told me about us Hollinsheads?

I felt as if a landmark had been obliterated from my life. I was melancholy for the inside of a day. He was more than a landmark; I felt as if he had been some sort of support. It is hard to describe; there was no sense in it. A problem had been looming all my life; but it was as if I had believed that one day, as if by magic, Inspector Brunt would materialize over some windswept brow and solve everything. There were secrets, mysteries in my life — and they had died with him.

And, oddly — for my reading these days was leading me into a phase of free-thinking and materialism — I felt a queer twist of conscience. In every interview I had had with Inspector Brunt—even, latterly, in this sitting-room—I had ultimately (and successfully) misled him. In my new brave agnosticism I was open-minded about any talk of after-life. Was there some plane on which Thomas Brunt now knew the answer to all things? And if he did, did he forgive me?

I had to admit to myself now that somewhere at the back of my mind there had lain the hope, growing thinner with the passing of time, that one day I would run into Mr Brunt again, and he would be in a position to tell me everything. Now that could not be. If ever I were to know the full tale of Mr Fred, it would have to be from some other source. But, these days, whole weeks could go by without my thoughts tracking back to Kiln Farm.

My relations with my mother during these years were unfilial and unrewarding, but they were saved from being downright bad because, without any declaration of intent, we kept largely out of each other's way. I can now see it as the natural sequence, but I sometimes thought it odd that she should have so little room for me, because of all the family, mine was the only lifestyle to which she might have aspired. Mine was the only home where there were space, newness and possessions worthy of respect. Lilian, doomed to be lower bourgeoise, put every last effort into aping some unattainable stratum of higher bourgeoisie. In her house, furniture, cushions and perpetual calendars were things which, ideally, no one ever touched. It would have needed the invective of Lady Marsden to do justice to Lilian. She and I got on together excellently during the first half-hour of our infrequent meetings.

Emily and her Ollerenshaw had now left the farm and were living in a quarryman's cottage in Waterlow—a hovel which they had neither the money, the know-how nor apparently the desire to improve. And yet my mother seemed happy enough to spend hours with them, perhaps because it did at least get her away from Kiln Farm, on which Thomas was now struggling not to starve, in company with a wife from Over Haddon way who always gave the impression that she was on the verge of leaving him. I think he always believed that she was about to, but she never did.

Walter and Jack, the youngest of all, were away overseas. When they remembered, they sent Christmas cards, which had nearly always arrived by February. Caroline, who had once wept over a road-skimming stone, had come back from her nursing in France to qualify into a teaching theatre-sister. She ran to a flat in West Didsbury and told us nothing about her private life. But there was a strong aura of the hyper-amoral about it, which she did her cunning best to nourish.

Stanley, still a bachelor, had come out of the Navy, in which he had served for some years on a reserve, and was in a semi-skilled job in the north-east, which cannot have paid him much, but which seemed to satisfy him. He could still talk with high intelligence, but there seemed little in his record to suggest that he had ever done anything intelligent. Also he drank too much, and depended on it.

We were an undistinguished family, with an average scatter. There was nothing really to unite us; and I can see no reason, other than novelettish sentiment, why we ought to be more united than we were. When we came together, we talked very little about old family history. Lilian loathed any mention of it, fearful of any reminder tracking behind her to Derby. The younger ones exchanged bored glances if ever we started: it had made little real impact on Emily and Caroline, none at all on the youngest. Only Stanley and I shared the bond of Mr Fred, and by now we had nothing new to tell each other. It follows that none of us would have dreamed of talking about our childhood to our mother. As the central force in the family she had done nothing constructive for us since my father had died. Though in intent she was naturally matriarchal, this mostly took the form of acidulous opposition to anything that was happening around her. She did not always express this in words, but one was always conscious of it. She began to spend more and more of her time in reading—mostly romances of the type in which she probably saw herself transmuted into a Lady Marsden. Lady Marsden would have laughed them to scorn.

She had no rapport with any of us. She quarrelled incessantly with Thomas's wife at the farm. Least of all did she quarrel with Emily in her slum; perhaps because Emily would have aroused the last vestige of compassion in anyone.

It was from Thomas that the suggestion came, inspired I am sure by his ever-menacing wife, that my mother should spend a fair portion of each year with each of those of us who had a home to offer her. She refused outright at first. Kiln Farm was her home and it was callous of anyone to uproot her, even for a couple of weeks. It was pathetic how tenaciously she clung to something that she must have detested. My children always looked forward to her visits, though I cannot think why. She never approached the grandmother's prerogative of spoiling them. She had no repertoire with which to entertain them. Maybe it was simply because she was different. When she came, it was a change.

We always got on well together, my mother and I, for the first ten minutes of any of her visits: when she was sitting with her first cup of tea, before she had taken her hat off. After that, there was always some stricture between us. I was prepared to do what I could for her. I honestly think that she tried to be on her best behaviour when she was in Bakewell. But there was an obstacle, and

I am sure that it arose from the things that neither of us dared mention to each other. Sometimes I had to fight an intense compulsion to do so — but I dared not broach the fateful syllable. It was always a relief to have John or one of the children in the room with us, because their presence inhibited the temptation. Sometimes I would switch on our three-valve radio-set and listen to something that I did not particularly want to hear — or that was practically inaudible — simply to have a centre of concentration that would keep my mind from spiralling down into the ever-present oppression.

She came to stay with us one autumn about six years after I had met Inspector Brunt at the dinner. Katherine was seven, young John Stanley was four. We went through the usual phases. I paraded what we had that was new to her: a cabinet gramophone, a set of watercolours by Wilson Steer, a new electric vacuum-cleaner. She contemplated these things with her customary refusal to take them in. The children rushed to show her their new talents and acquisitions and seemed not at all put off that her keenest interest was no more than perfunctory.

But what made her present visit even less bearable than previous ones was that during the last few months there had broken out a series of vicious attacks on children of about Katherine's age. A girl of nine, walking home from school along the Buxton road, had been seen getting into an open touring car that had stopped at the wayside — and had not arrived home that night. Her body had been found, sadistically molested, in a rubble hollow off the steep road up to Sheldon. Another child, several years younger, had actually been spirited away from a town street, where she had been playing in broad daylight on the pavement outside her own home. So far no trace of her had been found. There was another case in which two girls of seven or eight had set out together to go to Sunday School in the village of Great Longstone, but only one arrived. Her friend was hardly capable of giving a coherent account, but it seemed that Mavis had gone off to show a man the way to Shortlands Farm. Alice, obedient to lessons firmly drilled at home, had waited on the corner for Mavis to come back—which Mavis never did. When they found Mavis, she had not been ravished sexually—but her skull was broken.

And there was other evidence, from children of whom men had asked the way, but who had stuck to the instructions now being given in all the schools. My hopes were raised: there was great similarity between these crimes and those for which Mr Fred had been blamed—though I forced myself to remember that in this sort of obscenity, it might be difficult to be original. In the new wave children were being offered sweets, others sent to buy tobacco. Only nowadays it was always Liquorice All-Sorts or *Gold Flake* cigarettes.

All the same, my thoughts clung to wishful lines. It was hopeless asking children to judge the age of an adult, and the police were drawing such unpromising clues as *quite old—a grown man—wearing a porkpie hat—about seventy—about thirty-five—about sixty*. The resultant pen-portrait that got into the local press was less than definitive.

But if this were the man who had operated in Mr Fred's day, might he perhaps have held his horses ever since then, petrified with fear at what had happened to Mr Fred? Would a man as perverted as that, could he, have held his horses for close on twenty years? Might he perhaps have gone to prison for some other offence, round about that time? That was the sort of optimistic improbability with which my mind played. I knew there was no sense in it, yet I could not stop my brain from reeling round the possibilities until it nearly drove me distracted. I even did mental arithmetic to work out the possible age-range of a man who could have been guilty of both cycles of crime.

That was the form of mental torture that I was undergoing at the time my mother came. Additionally, I was in an almost insane state of fear about Katherine. She was so exactly of the right age, so naively attractive, so unsuspicious, so trusting. I gave way to a wave of superstition. Isn't that often so at times of real stress? I took to accompanying her to school and meeting her out, mornings and afternoons, even though the distance was short, she had no dangerous roads to cross and she always went and came in company with thoroughly reliable older girls; and there were always plenty of other mothers about. I would not even allow her to go alone to play in a neighbour's garden two houses away: I had to see her through the gate.

My mother watched my precautions in an expressionless silence. I sensed, or thought I could sense, her cynicism. We did not speak to each other about the man in the porkpie hat. But the days had gone now when no newspaper was taken at Kiln Farm, and she was nowaday an avid reader. I looked at her covertly in the evening sometimes and wondered what she was thinking. It was impossible that her mind was not being carried back to Mr Fred. Was she also making hopeful calculations that would have exonerated him? Or did she know beyond any doubt that Mr Fred had been guilty? Had she remained loyal to him while he was on the run, though she was under no illusions about his past? Just what had happened, that night that she had had Brindle with her?

The subject remained taboo between us. Something inside me was pressing me to bring it up: a new torture. And then something happened to force my hand.

John was out one evening, visiting a house that was to be put on sale, and whose owner was never home in the daytime. I had put the children to bed. The accumulator was so weak that I could not escape through the wireless. I was doing some desultory mending. My mother was reading a serial instalment in *Red Letter*, which I ordered specially for her when she was with us. Someone came to the door, and it was a detective-constable in plain clothes who was making door-to-door enquiries. Police frustration had reached the stage at which random items of remote likeliness were being studied: things children had said to each other, anything that might have been talked of in a playground, apparent irrelevances that teachers or parents had picked up.

And what a contrast this man was to Inspector Brunt! He was young, sleekly groomed enough to have sung with a dance-band. He had an easy manner — though he seemed to credit a woman of my age with no ideas of my own at all. I was not able to tell him anything useful and I gained no information from him. In spite of my mother's presence, silent in her corner, I asked direct questions about the state of their investigation.

After he had gone I was bound to speak to my mother about *Porkpie*. It would have been unnatural to have continued to sheer off the subject. I opened with the enlightened thought that it was a dreadful business.

'There'll always be men like that about,' she said.

'I know — but it's beyond my understanding, all the same. I'm frantic when I think that Katherine —'

'If you ask me, you're making a fool of yourself there.'

I was not surprised at her derisive tone. It was common in her attitude to anything to do with me. But I was surprised by her decisiveness. She had obviously been watching and weighing my every reaction — yet keeping her conclusions to herself.

'She hasn't to go more than a couple of hundred yards from the house, and the road's busy. There are always plenty of responsible people about. If you ask me, you're making a fool of the child. She's intelligent. She's been told to take double care. You know she'll do nothing silly. The way you keep on her shadow, you'll have the other children plaguing her to death.'

She looked at me with her frigid, satisfied conviction that she was being objective.

'But I suppose you suffer from a long memory,' she added.

Was this my cue? The room seemed to rock with me. Household objects seemed to be observing me in the same critical spirit as my mother.

'You mean Mr Fred?' my voice said.

She simply continued to look at me, as if she hated me for having been involved at all with Mr Fred.

'I know they said things about Mr Fred,' I said. 'I never knew whether they were true or not.'

I had hoped that this would be enough—that she would now have to say something. She went on studying me as if I were some alien body that had crept out of her womb.

'Did *you* believe those things about Mr Fred?' I plunged directly.

'Did *I* believe them? You damned nearly put yourself in a position to find out.'

A wave of adrenalin bristled over me. My lumbar regions felt heavy.

'What do you mean?'

'What do I mean. You know very well what I mean. William heard you.'

'William heard me?'

For a moment this meant nothing to me. Then I remembered how William had stood near us, that afternoon when Mr Fred had asked me to buy him the tobacco. As soon as Mr Fred saw that William was silently watching us, he gave me the fivepence and told me to go away. I could not think of anything that either of us said that might have upset William. He hadn't been standing

near enough to have heard much—could have heard
nothing clearly. But he had been worried. I remembered
that Stanley had told me that, after my father's funeral.

But if William thought he had heard something
untoward, and had said something at home about
it—which was extremely unlike him—why had nothing
been said to me? If they thought that I was in danger, why
had they done nothing about it?

'I don't know what you're talking about,' I said.

'No, well, if you're as ignorant as that, it would be well
to stay so.'

'Come, Mother, you're treating me as if *I* were some
sort of criminal.'

'You'd have done anything he asked you.'

'All he did ask me was to buy him an ounce of *Prince of
Wales*.'

'Yes. And you did. And you told lies to Inspector Brunt
about it. And *I* took it to Fred Needham. And he said I
was to thank you for it. Well—I've done that now. I've
thanked you for it.'

She spoke as if the whole trouble had been precipitated
by something that I had done. I began to wonder about
her mental state—but without sympathy.

'Better late than never,' I said, in a tone as bitter as
hers. 'And I still don't know what crime I'm supposed to
have committed.'

'You make me sick.'

'Obviously. Obviously I've had this emetic quality for
years, as far as you're concerned. I don't know why.'

'William heard you fixing with Fred Needham for you
to bring him his tobacco, and then he was going to show
you the place where he was hiding out.'

I remembered that now.

*Would you like to know a secret, Kathy . . . Would you
like to come and see where I live? . . . It isn't much of a
place, but I've got it cosy . . . You'll be surprised. But you*

must promise me that you'll never tell a soul . . .

'You know what would have happened, don't you, if you'd let him take you there? And you'd have gone with him, wouldn't you? It was the look in your eyes that said so. Yes, my girl — William told me that: *William*. It was plain enough for even him to see and recognize.'

There was about her a certain ugliness. She had always had the physical frame of a handsome woman, and there was no kind of aesthetic imbalance in her face. But it was an ugliness of attitude, that had taken possession of her eyes, brought down the corners of her mouth, affected even the tenor of her breathing.

'You'd have done anything he asked, wouldn't you? Disgusting things! And if you'd done the slightest thing to thwart him, if he'd lost his temper with you, he'd have killed you.'

Had he made her do disgusting things in her time? The thought revolted me. But there was something else uppermost in my mind; and my gooseflesh resolved into a body-suffusing flush.

'You knew all this about him — and did nothing to protect me?'

From emotional chaos she reverted into normal anger. Normal anger was easier to deal with, because I could give anger back.

'No! I did not know this about him! I did not know until it was too late to be worth knowing. I had heard what people said, and I rejected it — as you in your heart of hearts wish you could reject it now. William did not tell me what he had heard, not until we were crossing those pitch-dark fields on that last night. Only then did he open his mouth to me. And only then did I see the truth.'

'But I don't know what William could possibly have told you. I don't know what William could possibly have known. There was not a single word said, either by Mr Fred or by me, that could have given William a bad impression. Unless — oh, Mother! — you know how slow on the uptake William could be: he may have misunderstood something.'

'He misunderstood nothing. He told me what had been said, word for word, more or less. It amounted to what you've agreed to. You can say there was nothing objectionable in it, but for me — oh, I'll never explain to you! Why should I bother? It was in that moment that I saw the light. Let's say, rather, I saw the darkness. For the first time, I saw that people were telling the truth. Fred Needham was not on the run for nothing. I felt about you as you do about your Katherine —'

But that was not the whole story. I saw some light too. I had been reading Henry Williamson's *Tarka* and my blood had been frozen by the scene where Tarka had savagely drowned her own daughter because there was only a single dog-otter in the vicinity. I will not say that she was prompted only by jealousy of me. But I knew that jealousy had entered into it.

'So you told William to kill him.'

'I did not tell William to kill him.'

'Perhaps you did not say it in so many words — but you let him see that you wanted him to be killed.'

'Nothing of the kind.'

But I was beginning to see everything with devastating clarity.

'William left the house without the gun. I saw that myself. He came back in to get it. I remember how sheepish he looked. And Lilian gave evidence in court that that was what had happened. Lilian did not know that it had happened because of you. If the court had known that —'

'You have no right to speak to me like this. You have no right to think such things. I am going up to bed.'

I was still crying that evening when John came home. He

was concerned to find me in distress, but when he found out the cause of it, he did not try to placate me with gentleness. He was never quite himself when my mother was staying with us. And this time it was too much for him that it should be Mr Fred again—Mr Fred, who had eaten two decades out of my life.

'And *she* was responsible,' I said. 'But for *her*—'

'But for her? Aren't you still being too kind to her, Kathy? Don't you see: she was the one who had the dog. The dog was where the shot was fired. She sent William back indoors to get the gun; to get the gun to give to her. You saw her holding the gun afterwards, didn't you? You assumed that she had relieved your brother of it so that he could deal with the animal. Don't you think you might have been mistaken about that?'

'I'd be ready to believe it,' I said. 'It fits some of the facts—but for one thing. She'd never have let them hang my brother. And he would have spoken up, wouldn't he?'

'Who is to know what might have gone on in a mind like his? Who is to know what his brain would have made of it, under lock and key, cowed, bullied by policemen, swamped by wigs and gowns and solemn silences? Do you think he's the first innocent man to have been hanged because he was too confused to defend himself?'

'All this is supposition, John. I still can't believe that my mother—'

'She was an ordinary woman, Kathy. She had nine children and a difficult husband. When she saw the shadow of the noose—and a way of escape that cost her no more than the life of a halfwit son whom she had borne by a perverted murderer—'

'Oh, John—'

'Face the facts, Kathy—and try to forget them from now on.'

My mother died within the next twelve months. I was too

late at Kiln Farm to hear any last words from her. Only Thomas and his wife had been there at the time. I asked if she had said anything—I could not bring myself to be more specific. They had nothing to tell me.

I went to the graveside, my mind peopled with figures she had cut at phases in her life. There is no point in trying to revive them all here. I tried to find reasons for existence—and found none. Why should there be reasons?

Stanley had come down from Newcastle. This time even Lilian was here. I had not brought my children. At the end of the afternoon, after the serving of the customary tea, I wanted to get away quickly, before anyone started small-talk about family history.

But John had somehow contrived to disappear, saying nothing to me about where we were going. Stanley crept up to the side of my chair in the fashion he had had when we were exchanging secret information a quarter of a century ago.

'The more it changes, as the French say—'

But nothing had stayed the same. The shape of the room was not altered, but that was too indistinctive to give character. Thomas—or, more truthfully, his wife—had redecorated the house to their own liking: prints given free with the women's magazines, of girls in 1920ish hats hugging spaniels to their cheeks.

John was more than an hour away. When he came back, his trouser-legs were scuffed and chalky. There was mud over the laceholes of his shoes. He had hidden his raincoat in the back of the car before coming into the house. He told me about it as he drove us home.

'I felt I had to look. Goodness knows when we shall ever be up here again. It can't be too far hence for my taste. But there was something I've wanted to know—something that has always puzzled me—as I know that it puzzled Tom Brunt. Where had Needham made his hide-out?

How had it been so successful? My own private theory had been that one of those old houses round your Granny Smailes's crossroads had had a cellar. Perhaps it could still be found among those overgrown foundations. I thought I'd poke around, see if I could find it. Though I don't know what hope I thought I'd have, where the cream of the county CID had failed. The uncanny thing is that there's barely a vestige of Granny Smailes's house left now, either. Hardly a stone. You can just about see where the footings were. But there's still mint growing about profusely—as I've heard you describe. Otherwise nothing. I expect your brother Thomas has used the stones to repair his barns: cannibalizing is the word they use nowadays.'

We had skirted Buxton and were swinging down from Sherbrook towards Ashwood Dale along what they called the Duke's Drive. We drove under the great railway viaduct, a structure that I found not merely awe-inspiring, but positively frightening: a monument to man's scorn for obstacles.

'There were no signs of cellars anywhere. I was being foolishly optimistic. They didn't build that sort of cottage with cellars. So it had to be the kiln. And I'd always had a theory about that too. You know how the thing is built into the hillside, with the chimney emerging at ground-level behind it. Tom Brunt had had a go at that chimney. I remember seeing smoke coming out of it, once when I was in my teens and walking your hills—That was to push Needham out, if he'd happened to have crawled up there. But it didn't work: either because Needham wasn't there, or because he had a refuge from the smoke. Suppose there was a chamber, built halfway up, out of the stack. The draught would carry the smoke up and away. I came across the same sort of thing once on a parcel of land I surveyed for a client out at Ladmanlow. Some of the old Derbyshire farmers went in for that kind of construction a

couple of centuries ago. They trusted no one. They never
knew when they might have something, or someone—or
themselves—to hide. I managed to get a foothold in that
chimney. And there was a little room, about eight feet by
eight. A lime deposit was already beginning to scale the
few things that had been left there. There was not much:
a table, a chair, a tableknife with a groove in its handle,
as if it had been laid against the edge of a hot frying-pan.
A fork with a twisted tine. And an old tin: a flat old
tobacco-tin. No, I'm sorry, it wasn't even *Prince of
Wales*. It was *St Julien*. He'd kept a few scraps of paper in
there: a letter or two, and a pathetic sort of
diary—nothing continuous—just sporadic notes and
thoughts, written on the back of old wrapping paper,
even on the inside of an old match-box.'

We were climbing Topley Pike in bottom gear, the
engine singing. Over to the east stretched a patchwork of
irregular walled fields.

'Old Fred Needham, you know, wrote in rather a
beautiful hand: copybook elegance. I won't quote what
he wrote. There was implicit evidence that could sub-
stantiate many of the things that were said about him—if
you wanted it to. I burned the lot. It would do no one any
good for strangers to go mulling over it again. There was
one note that might interest you. *Begged Hetty today to
shoot me if she sees me being taken. I could not face that.*
I burned it, alongside the rest. But I thought it might
help you to feel better.'

We dropped down through Taddington Dale to the
green leafiness of Ashford-in-the-Water. I have often felt
that the High Peak takes on a kinder, milder, lusher look
as one coasts down into Bakewell.

I am in my eighties. I have five sturdy grandchildren,
whom I consider beautiful. My own children went to
universities, married happily. I have not told them the

story of Mr Fred. This is for them to read when I can no longer be taxed with questions about it.

I hope, prosperous and adventurous as they are, that they will reflect for a moment or so that they would not be here but for Hetty Price and Will Hollinshead: and that Mr Fred had something to do with it.